PENGUIN MODERN CLASSICS

APOCRYPHAL STORIES

Karel Čapek, the Czech novelist, dramatist and essayist, was born in Bohemia in 1890. Having studied philosophy in Prague, Berlin and Paris, he travelled extensively in Europe. He worked as a journalist throughout his life, writing prolifically.

Among his plays are *The Macropoulos Secret* (1927), *Adam the Creator* (1927), *The Mother* (1938) and his most famous, *R.U.R.* ('Rossum's Universal Robots') (1920). He also wrote numerous books on travel, such as *Letters from England* (1924), and diverse essays, such as *Power and Glory* (1938). As well as the *Apocryphal Stories*, he wrote the novel *An Atomic Phantasy* (1938). He died in 1938.

Apocryphal Stories

KAREL ČAPEK

TRANSLATED BY
DORA ROUND

PENGUIN BOOKS

Penguin Books Ltd, Harmondsworth, Middlesex, England
Penguin Books Inc., 7110 Ambassador Road, Baltimore, Maryland 21207, U.S.A.
Penguin Books Australia Ltd, Ringwood, Victoria, Australia
Penguin Books Canada Ltd, 41 Steelcase Road West, Markham, Ontario, Canada
Penguin Books (N.Z.) Ltd, 182–190 Wairau Road, Auckland 10, New Zealand

—

Translated from the Czech original *Kniha apokryfů*, Dorovy, Prague, 1945
This translation first published in England in 1949
Published in Penguin Books 1975

—

Made and printed in Great Britain by
Hazell Watson & Viney Ltd, Aylesbury, Bucks
Set in Linotype Juliana

Contents

CONTENTS

The Punishment of Prometheus

WITH much coughing and clearing of throats and after prolonged proceedings for the collection of evidence, the extraordinary Senate betook itself to the meeting, which was held in the shade of the sacred olive grove.

'Well, gentlemen,' yawned Hypometheus, the president of the Senate, 'what a confoundedly long time all this has taken! I think I hardly need to sum up; however, to obviate any formal objections – The accused, Prometheus, a citizen of this place, being summoned before the court on a charge of inventing fire and thereby – hm, hm – upsetting the existing order of things, confessed, firstly, that he actually invented fire; further, that he is able to produce the same at any time by the action called kindling; thirdly, that he did not keep this mystery – this shocking phenomenon – secret or report it to the appropriate authority but deliberately revealed it, in fact handed it over to the use of unauthorized persons, as is proved by the evidence of the persons concerned, whom we have just interrogated. I think that is all and that we can proceed at once to declare him guilty and to pronounce the sentence.'

'Excuse me, Mr President,' objected the lay magistrate Apometheus, 'but I consider that in view of the importance of this extraordinary tribunal it would have been more suitable if we proceeded to pronounce judgement after deliberation and, so to speak, general discussion.'

'As you please, gentlemen,' assented the conciliatory

Hypometheus. 'The case is perfectly clear, but if any of you wish to make a remark, please do so.'

'I would venture to point out,' said Ametheus, a member of the tribunal, coughing primly, 'that in my opinion one aspect of the whole matter should be specially emphasized. Gentlemen, I am thinking of the religious aspect. I ask you, what is this fire? What is this kindled spark? As Prometheus himself admits, it is nothing other than lightning, and lightning, as we all know, is the expression of the extraordinary power of Zeus the Thunderer. Will you explain to me, gentlemen, how an ordinary fellow like Prometheus had access to this divine fire? By what right did he seize it? Where did he get it from? Prometheus has tried to persuade us that he simply invented it; but that is a silly excuse – if it were as simple and innocent as all that, why should not one of us have invented fire? I am convinced, gentlemen, that Prometheus simply stole this fire from our gods. His denial and prevarication do not mislead us. I would describe his crime as common theft on the one hand, and as the crime of blasphemy and sacrilege on the other. We are here to punish with the utmost severity this impious presumptuousness and to protect the sacred property of our national gods. That is all I wished to say,' concluded Ametheus, and blew his nose energetically on the corner of his chlamys.

'Well said,' agreed Hypometheus. 'Does anyone else wish to make a remark?'

'I ask your indulgence,' said Apometheus, 'but I cannot agree with the argument of my esteemed colleague. I watched how the said Prometheus kindled this fire; and I tell you frankly, gentlemen, that – between ourselves – there's absolutely nothing in it. The discovery of fire could have been made by any idler, loafer or goatherd; we ourselves did not happen upon it simply because a serious man hasn't the time and doesn't dream of playing about with stones to make fire. I assure my colleague Ametheus that these are quite ordinary natural forces which it is beneath the dignity of a thinking man, much less a god, to occupy himself with. In my opinion fire is too insignificant to affect in any way matters which are sacred to us all. But the case has another aspect, to which I must call the attention of my distinguished colleagues. It appears that fire is a very dangerous element, in fact even harmful. You have heard a number of witnesses who have deposed that in trying Prometheus's boyish invention they have suffered serious burns and in some cases even damage to property. Gentlemen, if through the fault of Prometheus the use of fire becomes general, which now, unfortunately, seems impossible to prevent, neither the property nor even the lives of any of us will be safe; and that, gentlemen, may mean the end of all civilization. It needs only the least carelessness – and at what will this mischief-working element stop? Prometheus, gentlemen, has committed an act of criminal irresponsibility in bringing into the world so harmful a thing. I should describe his crime as the causing of grievous bodily harm and endangering the public safety. In view of this I am in favour of a life sentence of imprisonment with a hard pallet and manacles. I have finished, Mr President.'

'You are perfectly right, sir,' grunted Hypometheus. 'And I would just like to say, gentlemen, what did we need this fire for, anyway? Did our forefathers use fire? To invent such a thing is simply disrespect to the inherited order, it is – hm, merely revolutionary activity. Playing about with fire, who ever heard of such a thing? And consider, gentlemen, what it leads to: people will relax by the fire, they will wallow in warmth and comfort instead of – well, instead of fighting and things like that. It can only lead to effeminacy, the degeneration of morals and – hm, general disorder and so on. In a word, something must be done against such unhealthy signs. The times are grave, very grave. That is all I wished to point out.'

'Most rightly said,' declared Antimetheus. 'We all certainly agree with our President that Prometheus's fire may have unforeseeable consequences. Gentlemen, do not let us conceal the fact from ourselves, it is a tremendous thing. To have fire in one's power – what new possibilities open out before one! I will only mention a few of them haphazard: to burn the enemy's crop, set fire to his olive groves and so on. In fire, gentlemen, our people have been given a new force and a new weapon; through fire we shall become almost equal to the gods,' whispered Antimetheus, and suddenly exploded fiercely. 'I accuse Prometheus of having entrusted this divine and irresistible element of fire to shepherds and slaves, to the first comer; I accuse him of not giving it up into authorized hands which would have guarded it as a treasure of the state and governed by its means. I accuse Prometheus of thus being a dishonest trustee of the discovery of fire, which should be a secret of the priesthood. I accuse Prometheus,' shouted Antimetheus, carried away by emotion, 'of teaching even foreigners how to kindle fire! of not concealing it even from our enemies! Prometheus stole fire from us by giving it to everyone! I accuse Prometheus of high treason! I accuse him of conspiracy against the community!' His voice rose to a scream and he broke off, coughing. 'I propose the death sentence,' he managed to get out.

'Well, gentlemen,' said Hypometheus, 'does anyone else wish to speak? Then in the opinion of the court the accused Prometheus is found guilty firstly of the crime of blasphemy and sacrilege, secondly of the crime of inflicting grievous bodily harm, causing damage to the property of others and endangering the public safety, and thirdly of the crime of high treason. Gentlemen, I propose to pass sentence upon him either of life imprisonment, rendered more rigorous by hard pallet and manacles, or sentence of death. Ahm.'

'Or both,' said Ametheus thoughtfully, 'so as to comply with both proposals.'

'How do you mean, both sentences?' asked the president.

'I've just been thinking it over,' grunted Ametheus. 'Perhaps we could manage it like this ... condemn Prometheus to be chained to a rock for the rest of his life ... perhaps let vultures peck out his godless liver, does Your Excellency understand?'

'That would do,' said Hypometheus placidly. 'Gentlemen, that would be an exemplary punishment for such a – ahem – criminal eccentricity, wouldn't it? Has anyone any objection? Then the session is closed.'

*

'And why did you condemn Prometheus to death, Daddy?' Hypometheus's son, Epimetheus, asked him at supper.

'You wouldn't understand,' grunted Hypometheus, gnawing a leg of mutton as he spoke. 'Upon my word, this mutton tastes better roasted than raw; so you see, this fire is some use after all. It was for reasons of public interest, do you see? Where should we be if anyone who liked was allowed to come along with great, new inventions unpunished? See what I mean? But there's something this meat still needs – Ah, I've got it!' he exclaimed delightedly. 'Roast mutton ought to be salted and rubbed with garlic! That's the right way to do it! Now that is a real discovery! You know, a fellow like Prometheus would never have thought of that!'

(1932)

Times Aren't What They Were

It was quiet in front of the cave. The men had gone off early in the morning, waving their spears, towards the hills, where a herd of deer had been sighted; meanwhile the women were picking berries in the forest and their shrill cries and chatter could only be heard now and then; the children were mostly splashing down in the stream – and besides, who would have taken any notice of the grubby and mischievous little ragamuffins? So Johnny, the old cave man, dozed in the unusual quiet, in the soft October sunshine. To tell the truth he was snoring and his breath whistled in his nose, but he pretended not to be asleep but to be watching over the cave of his tribe and ruling it, as befits an old chief.

Old Mrs Johnny spread out a fresh bear skin and set about scraping it with a sharp flint. It had to be done thoroughly, span by span – and not the way that girl did it, thought old Mrs Johnny suddenly; the lazybones only gave it a lick and a promise and ran off to cuddle the children and romp with them – a skin like this, she thought, won't last a bit! it's too bad, they either handle them roughly or let them rot! but I shan't interfere if my son doesn't tell her himself. The truth is that girl doesn't know how to take care of nice things. And here's a hole pierced in the skin right in the middle of the back! My goodness me, thought the old lady in shocked astonishment, what butter-fingers stabbed this bear in the back? Why, it ruins the whole hide! My old man would never have done a thing like that. He always aimed at the neck and hit it –

'Ah ha,' yawned old Johnny at that moment and rubbed his eyes. 'Aren't they back yet?'

'Of course not,' grunted the old lady. 'You must wait.'

'Tcha,' sighed the old man and blinked sleepily. 'Of course not yourself! Oh, all right. And where are the women?'

'Shall I go and look for them?' snapped the old lady. 'You know they're lounging about somewhere –'

'Ahyaya,' yawned Johnny. 'They're lounging about somewhere. Instead of – instead of doing this or that – Well, well.'

*

There was silence. Old Mrs Johnny swiftly scraped the raw hide with angry concentration.

'I tell you,' said Johnny, scratching his back thoughtfully, 'you'll see, they won't bring anything back this time either. It stands to reason: with those good-for-nothing bone-headed spears of theirs. And I'm always saying to our son: look here, no bone is hard and firm enough to make spears out of! Why, even a woman like you must know that neither bone nor horn has the – well, the striking force. You hit a bone with it and you don't cut through bone with bone, do you? That's only sense. A stone spearhead, now – of course it's more work, but then, what an instrument it is! And what do you think our son said?'

'Yes,' said Mrs Johnny bitterly. 'You can't tell them anything nowadays.'

'I don't want to tell them anything,' said the old man crossly. 'But they won't even listen to advice! Yesterday I found such a lovely flat piece of flint under the rock over there. It only needed trimming a little round the edges to make it sharper and it would have been a spearhead, a beauty. So I brought it home and showed it to our son. "Look, here's a stone for you, what?" "So it is," he answered, "but what should I do with it, Dad?" "Why, bless me, it could be worked up into a spearhead," I said. "Nonsense, Dad," he said, "who'd bother about chipping and sharpening that? Why, we've whole heaps of that old junk in the cave and it's no use for anything! It won't hold on to the shaft, lash it how you may, so what can you do with it?" A lazy lot they are!' shouted the old man angrily. 'No one wants to trim a piece of flint properly these days, that's what it is! They just want to be comfortable! Of course a bone spearhead is made in the twinkling of an eye, but it breaks at once. That doesn't matter, our son says, you just make another and there you are. Well, perhaps, but where does that get you? A new spearhead every other minute! Who ever saw the like, tell me that! Why, a good flint spearhead used to last for ages and ages! But what I say is, just you wait! one day they'll be glad to return to our honest stone weapons! That's why I keep them whenever I find them: old arrows and hammers and flint knives. – And he calls it junk!'

The old man nearly choked with grief and rage.

'You know,' said Mrs Johnny to make him think of something else, 'it's just the same with these hides. "Mother," that girl says to me, "why on earth do you do all that scraping, it's such a lot of trouble! you try dressing the hide with ash, at least that doesn't stink." You'd teach me, would you?' the old lady burst out at her absent daughter-in-law. 'I know what I know! People have always scraped hides, and what hides they used to be! Of course, if it's too much trouble for you – That's why they're always inventing and trying out something new. – Dressing hides with ash, indeed! Who's ever heard of such a thing?'

'There you are,' yawned Johnny. '*Our* way of doing things isn't good enough for them. Oh no! And they say stone weapons are uncomfortable to the hand. Well, it's certainly true we didn't think very much about comfort! but nowadays – dear, dear, dear, mind you don't bruise your poor hands! I ask you, where's it all going to end? Take the present-day children. "Just leave them alone, grandad," our daughter-in-law says, "let them romp." Very well, but what are they going to grow up like?'

'If only it didn't make them so loutish,' lamented the old lady. 'They're ill bred, and that's the truth!'

'It's the fault of this modern education,' declared Old Johnny. 'And if just now and then I drop a word to our son he says: "Dad, you don't understand, times have changed, this is a different epoch. Why," he says, "even these bone weapons aren't the last word! some day people will discover a better material –" Now, you know, that's really beyond everything! As though anyone had ever seen any resistant material but stone, wood or bone! Why, even a silly woman like you must admit that – that – that it's absolutely outrageous!'

Mrs Johnny let her hands fall into her lap. 'Oh dear,' she said. 'Where can they get these absurd ideas from?'

'They say it's the latest fashion,' mumbled the toothless old man. 'I tell you, over yonder, four days' journey from here, a new tribe has moved in, a pack of foreigners, and our boy says that's what they're doing. So you see, our youngsters have got all this nonsense from them. These bone-headed weapons and all. They even – they even buy the stuff from them,' he shouted angrily, 'for our good hides! As if anything good ever came from foreigners!

Never have anything to do with foreign riff-raff. Why, that's the teaching handed down to us by our forefathers: when you see a foreigner, fall upon him and bash his head in without more ado. That's always been the rule: no palaver, just kill him. "Not a bit of it, Dad," says our son, "times have changed, we're beginning to exchange goods with them." Exchange goods! If I kill a man and take what he's got I get his goods and don't give him anything for them – so why exchange? "No, no, Dad," says our son, "You pay in human lives and it's a pity to waste them." So there you are: they say it's a waste of human lives. That's the modern view,' growled the old man with distaste: 'They're cowards, that's what they are! And how are so many people going to get enough to eat if they don't kill each other, tell me that? Why, elk are getting confoundedly scarce as it is! It's all very well not wanting to waste human lives; but they have no respect for tradition, they don't honour their forefathers and their parents. Everything's going to rack and ruin,' old Johnny burst out violently. 'The other day I saw one of these young whipper-snappers daubing clay on the wall of the cave in the likeness of a bison. I gave him a box on the ear, but our son said: "Let him be, why, the bison looks absolutely alive!" Now, that really is beyond everything! Who ever heard of wasting time like that? If you've not enough to do, boy, then trim a piece of flint, but don't paint bison on the wall! What's the use of such nonsense?'

Mrs Johnny pursed up her lips severely. 'If it were only bison,' she let drop after a moment.

'What do you mean?' asked the old man.

'Oh nothing,' said Mrs Johnny defensively, 'I'm ashamed to talk about it ... Well, if you must know,' she said with sudden decision, 'this morning I found ... in the

cave ... a piece of mammoth tusk. It was carved like ...
like a naked woman. Breasts and all.'

'You don't mean it!' said the old man, astonished. 'And
who carved it?'

Mrs Johnny shrugged her shoulders with a shocked
expression on her face. 'Who knows? One of the youngsters, I suppose. I threw it into the fire, but – Such breasts
it had! Fi!'

'Things can't go on like this,' said old Johnny, getting
the words out with difficulty. 'It's perverse! You know, it
all comes of their carving all manner of things out of bone!
We never thought of doing anything so shameless because
you simply couldn't do it in flint. This is what it leads
to! These are their vaunted discoveries! They must always
be inventing something, always starting something new,
till they bring everything to rack and ruin. And you mark
my words,' cried Johnny the cave man with prophetic
illumination, 'the whole thing won't last much longer!'

(1931)

As in the Good Old Days

EUPATOR, a citizen of Thebes and a basket-maker, was sitting in his courtyard weaving his baskets when his neighbour Philagoros came hurrying along, shouting while he was still a long way off:

'Eupator, Eupator, leave your baskets and listen! Dreadful things are going on!'

'Whose house is burning?' asked Eupator, making as if to rise.

'It's worse than a fire,' said Philagoros. 'Do you know what's happened? They want to have our General Nikomachos up for trial! Some people say he's guilty of intriguing with the Thessalonians, and other people say he's accused of being mixed up with the Malcontents' Party. Come quickly, we're assembling in the market-place!'

'And what should I do there?' asked Eupator irresolutely.

'It's frightfully important,' said Philagoros. 'The place is full of speakers already; some of them say he's innocent and the others say he's guilty. Come and listen to them?'

'Wait a minute,' said Eupator, 'just while I finish this basket. And tell me, what is Nikomachos really guilty of?'

'People don't quite know,' said his neighbour. 'One says one thing and one says another, but the authorities haven't said anything, because it seems the inquiry isn't finished yet. But there was a fine to do in the market-place, you should have seen it! Some people shouting that Nikomachos is innocent —'

'Wait a minute; how can they be shouting that he's innocent when they don't know for certain what he's guilty of?'

'It doesn't matter; everyone's heard something and just talks about what he's heard. We've all got the right to talk about what we hear, haven't we? I believe Nikomachos was trying to betray us to the Thessalonians; someone there said so, and he said someone he knew had seen a letter. But one man said it was a plot against Nikomachos and that he knew a thing or two about it. They say the Government's involved in it. Are you listening, Eupator? The question now is –'

'Wait a minute,' said the basket-maker. 'The question now is, are the laws which we have given ourselves good or bad? Did anyone say anything about that in the market-place?'

'No, but that's not what it's about; it's about Nikomachos.'

'And does anyone in the market-place say that the officials who are examining Nikomachos are bad and unjust?'

'No, nothing was said about that at all.'

'Then what was said?'

'Why, I'm telling you: about whether Nikomachos is guilty or innocent.'

'Listen, Philagoros, if your wife were quarrelling with the butcher because she said he hadn't given her a good pound's weight of meat, what would you do?'

'Help my wife.'

'No, no. You'd look to see if the butcher had good weights.'

'I know that without your telling me, man.'

'There you see. And then you'd look if his scales were in order.'

'You don't need to tell me that either, Eupator.'

'I'm glad. And if weights and scales were in order, you'd look how much the piece of meat weighed and you'd see at once who was right, the butcher or your wife. It's strange, Philagoros, that people are much more sensible when it's a case of their own piece of meat than when it's a case of public affairs. Is Nikomachos guilty or innocent? The scales will show, if they are in order. But if they are to weigh correctly you mustn't blow on either scale to make it incline to one side or the other. Why, do you maintain that the officials who are trying the case of Nikomachos are shady characters or something like that?'

'No one said that, Eupator.'

'I thought you didn't believe them; but if you have no reason not to believe them, why on earth do you blow on the scales? Either it's because you don't mind whether the truth comes to light or it's because you only want to split up into two parties and quarrel. Confound you all, Philagoros; I don't know if Nikomachos is guilty, but you are all damnably guilty of trying to interfere with the course of justice. It's amazing how bad the osiers are this year; they bend like cords but they aren't firm at all. We need some warmer weather, Philagoros; but that is in the hands of the gods, not in ours.'

(1926)

Thersites

It was night, and the men of Achaia sat huddled close to their camp fires.

'The meat wasn't fit to eat again,' said Thersites, picking his teeth. 'I'm surprised you put up with it, Achaians. I bet *they* had at least roast sucking lamb; but of course, for us old soldiers stinking goat flesh is good enough. Why, boys, when I remember the mutton at home in Greece –'

'Shut up, Thersites,' grunted Father Eupator. 'There's a war on.'

'War,' said Thersites. 'I ask you, do you call this war? Hanging about here for ten years wasting time and doing nothing? I tell you what it is, boys, it's not a war at all, it's just that the officers and gentlemen commanding us have been having a holiday abroad at government expense; and we old soldiers have to look on open-mouthed while some young puppy, some jackanapes, some mother's darling stalks about the camp giving himself airs and swaggering with his shield. That's what it is.'

'You mean Achilles, son of Peleus,' said young Laomedon.

'Him or another,' declared Thersites. 'Anyone with eyes in his head can see whom the description fits. No one's going to persuade us that if it had really been a question of conquering this wretched Troy we shouldn't have had it long ago. Why, if we gave one good sneeze it would be a heap of ruins. Then why don't we make an attack on the main gate? You know, a thoroughly impressive storming

22

action with shouting, threats and the singing of war songs
– it would end the war in no time.'

'Hm,' murmured Eupator meditatively, 'Troy won't fall
for shouting.'

'A fat lot you know about it,' said Thersites. 'Every
child knows that the Trojans are gutless, mangy cowards
and riff-raff. We should just throw out our chests and
tell them straight out the kind of people we Greeks are !
You'd see how they'd come crawling and begging for
mercy ! It would be enough now and then to attack the
Trojan women when they go to draw water in the evening –'

'You can't attack women,' said Hippodamos of Megara,
shrugging his shoulders. 'It's not done, Thersites.'

'There's a war on,' declared Thersites aggressively.
'You're a nice patriot, Hippodamos ! D'you think we shall
win this war just by my lord Achilles staging a public
fight with that clumsy bull-in-a-china-shop Hector once
every three months? Why, men, those two have got it all
agreed and worked out to a T; their duels are solo numbers
staged to make all these poor stupid coves think they are
fighting for *them* ! Hi, Troy ! hi, Hellas ! come and stare
at the heroes ! And we others are nothing, nobody cares
two hoots for *our* sufferings, not a dog barks when *we* go
by. I'll tell you something, Achaians : Achilles only plays
the hero so as to skim all the cream for himself and deprive the rest of us of martial credit; he wants people to
talk about him all the time as if he were everything and
the rest of us just dirt. That's how it is, boys. And this war
is dragging on and on just so that Mr Achilles can puff
himself up like some sort of hero. I'm surprised you don't
see it.'

'I say, Thersites,' said young Laomedon, 'what's Achilles
done to you, after all?'

'Me? Nothing at all,' snapped Thersites indignantly. 'What do I care about him? As a matter of fact, I don't even speak to him; but everyone's fed up to the teeth with the airs the fellow gives himself. For instance, that sulking in his tent. We're living at an historic moment when the honour of our Hellas is at stake; the whole world is watching us – and what does Mr Hero do? Stalks into his tent and says he won't fight. Are we to slave for him and save the historic moment and the honour of Hellas? But that's how it is: when there's a disagreeable job to be done Achilles crawls into his tent and poses as an insulted hero. Pff, play-acting! That's what your national heroes are! Just cowards!'

'I don't know, Thersites,' said the prudent Eupator. 'They say Achilles is terribly insulted because Agamemnon sent that slave girl of his, Briseis or Chryseis or whatever her name is, back to her parents. Achilles is making it a matter of prestige, but I think he really loved the girl. That wouldn't be play-acting.'

'You won't put that over on *me*,' said Thersites. 'I know all about it. Agememnon just took the girl away from him, didn't he? We all know he's got stacks of looted jewels and is as bad as a tom cat about women – I'm fed up with all these women; it was all because of that trollop Helen that the war began, and now this business. Did you hear that Helen's carrying on with Hector, now? I tell you, every man in Troy has been with that woman, even that old boy with one foot in the grave, that doddering old Priam. And have we got to suffer and fight here for the sake of a hussy like that? No, thanks!'

'They say,' remarked young Laomedon hesitatingly, 'that Helen is very beautiful.'

'They said so,' said Thersites scornfully. 'She's too old by a long chalk and an unparalleled slut into the bargain.

I wouldn't give a sack of beans for her. Boys, d'you know what I wish that stupid Menelaus? I wish we may win this war for him and that he may get his Helen back. All Helen's beauty is only a legend, a swindle and a little bit of make-up.'

'And we Greeks, Thersites,' said Hippodamus, 'are we fighting for a mere legend?'

'My dear Hippodamus,' said Thersites, 'you don't seem to see. We Hellenes are fighting, firstly, so that the old fox, Agamemnon, may get a sack full of booty; secondly, so that the coxcomb Achilles may satisfy his inordinate ambition; thirdly, so that the trickster Odysseus may cheat us over the war supplies; and finally, so that a certain corrupt balladmonger, Homer or whatever the fellow's name is, may glorify the greatest traitors to the Greek nation for a couple of dirty groats and vilify or at least ignore the true, modest, self-sacrificing Achaian heroes, who are yourselves. That's how it is, Hippodamus.'

'The greatest traitors,' repeated Eupator; 'the word is a bit strong, Thersites.'

'Well, if you want to know,' Thersites burst out and lowered his voice, 'I have proof of their treachery. It's terrible; I won't tell you all I know, but just put this in your pipe and smoke it: we've been sold. Of course, you must know it yourselves. Do you really believe that we Greeks, the bravest and most advanced nation on earth, would not long ago have conquered this Trojan dunghill and mopped up the beggars and hooligans in Ilium if we hadn't been betrayed for donkey's years? Do you, Eupator, consider us Achaians such cowardly dogs that we shouldn't have polished off this dirty town of Troy long ago? Are the Trojans better soldiers than we? Listen to me, Eupator, if that's what you think then you can't be a Greek, you must be an Epirot or a Thracian. The true

Greek of antiquity must feel with grief that the slipshod way things are being run is an absolute disgrace.'

'It is true,' said Hippodamus thoughtfully, 'that this war is dragging on confoundedly.'

'There, you see!' exclaimed Thersites. 'And I'll tell you why: because the Trojans have their Fifth Columnists and collaborators among us. Perhaps you know who I mean.'

'Who?' asked Eupator gravely. 'You must finish now, Thersites, since you've begun.'

'I don't like saying it,' protested Thersites. 'You Greeks know that I never gossip; but as it's in the public interest, I'll tell you a dreadful thing. One time I was talking to some good and valiant Greeks; I was talking like a patriotic man about the war and about the enemy, and with my open Greek nature I was saying that the Trojans, our mortal and savage enemies, are a pack of cowards, criminals, knaves, scoundrels and rats, and that their Priam is an old dodderer and their Hector a villain. You admit, Achaians, that that is the correct opinion for a Greek. And suddenly Agememnon stepped out from the shadow of a tent – he isn't even ashamed to eaves-drop! – and said: "Softly, Thersites; the Trojans are good soldiers, Priam is a fine old man and Hector is a hero." Then he turned on his heel and disappeared before I could snub him as he deserved. Friends, I was flabbergasted. Oho, I said to myself, so that's the way the wind blows! Now we know who is spreading subversive talk, des-pondency and enemy propaganda in our camp! How are we going to win the war when these dirty Trojans have their own people, their collaborators, in our midst, yes, worse than that, actually at General Headquarters? And do you think, Achaians, that a traitor like that is doing his subversive work for nothing? Not on your life. He wouldn't praise our national enemies to the skies for nothing; he must have been paid a mint of money by the Trojans. Just you think it out a bit, boys: the war is being deliberately prolonged, Achilles was purposely insulted, you hear nothing but complaints and grumbling in our army, lack of discipline is spreading everywhere – in fact, it's simply a nest of incompetents and a den of thieves. Everyone you look at is a traitor, a mercenary, a foreigner or a political jobber. And when one exposes their tricks they say one's a fault-finder and a disruptive element. That's what a person like me gets when he tries, without looking to the right or to the left, to serve his nation and its honour and glory! That's what we ancient Greeks have come to! To think we aren't choked by all this slime! Some day they will write of our time as of a period of the deepest national disgrace and subjection, infamy, pettiness and treachery, bondage and subversion, cowardice, corruption and moral rottenness –'

'We shall muddle through,' yawned Eupator. 'And I'm going to sleep. Good-night, chums.'

'Good-night,' said Thersites heartily and stretched himself out with enjoyment. 'We've had a nice old pow-wow this evening, haven't we?'

(1931)

Agathon, or Concerning Wisdom

THE members of the academy of Boeotia invited the philosopher Agathon from Athens to lecture to them on philosophy. Although Agathon was not an eminent orator he accepted the invitation so as to contribute as far as lay in his power to spreading the knowledge of philosophy, which, in the words of the historian, 'seemed to be on the decline'. On the appointed day he arrived at Boeotia, but it was still early; Agathon therefore walked round the city in the morning twilight and enjoyed the flight of the swallows above its roofs.

On the stroke of eight he betook himself to the lecture hall but found it almost empty; only five or six men sat on the benches. Agathon sat down in the lecturer's chair and resolved to wait a little until a greater number of listeners should come; in the meantime he opened the roll of parchment from which he intended to read, and scanned it.

This roll of parchment contained all the fundamental questions of philosophy; it began with the theory of cognition, defined truth, dismissed with crushing criticism all erroneous views, that is to say all the philosophy in the world except that of Agathon, and gave an outline of the highest ideas. When Agathon reached this point he raised his eyes; he saw that the full number of his listeners was nine; rage and grief filled his breast, and flinging the roll of parchment on to a table he began thus:

Ladies and Gentlemen,

or rather *andres Boiotikoi*, it does not seem as if your city had great interest in the lofty questions which we have on the programme. I know, men of Boeotia, that you are at the moment engaged in elections to the local council and that at such a time there is no place for wisdom nor even for reason; elections are the opportunity of the clever.

Here Agathon pulled himself up and thought a little. 'Wait a minute,' he began again. 'I have just let slip something which I had never considered before. I spoke three words: cleverness – reason – wisdom. I said it in anger. All three mean a certain intellectual ability; I feel that they have a completely different sense but I could hardly say in what they differ. Excuse me, I will go back to the programme in a minute; I must just explain these three words a little.

'This much is clear,' he went on after a pause. 'The opposite of cleverness is stupidity, while the opposite of reason is folly. But what is the opposite of wisdom! There are thoughts, gentlemen, which are not clever, for they are too simple, and are not reasonable, for they resemble folly, and which yet are wise. Wisdom does not resemble either reason or cleverness.

'Men of Boeotia, in everyday life you do not care a fig, as we say in Greek, for the definition of conceptions, and yet you distinguish them clearly. You say of someone that he is a clever thief; but you never talk of "a sensible thief" or "a wise thief". You praise your tailor for having reasonable prices, but you never say he has wise prices. There is obviously a certain difference which prevents you from mixing the words.

'If you say of someone that he is a clever farmer you clearly mean by that that he knows how to sell his goods well at market; if you say that he is a sensible farmer you probably mean that he manages his farm well; but if you call him a wise farmer you mean that he lives well, knows a great deal and can advise you sympathetically.

'Or let us assume that a clever politician may be a mountebank and do harm to the Republic; but a politician of sense is something that you only call a man who is able to direct matters in a praiseworthy manner to the public good; while a wise politician, gentlemen, as you all certainly know, is the kind of man who is called "the father of his country" or something like that; it is clear that wisdom is a quality which comes from the heart.

'When I say of someone that he is clever, I am thinking of a remarkable peculiarity; it is as though I said that a bee has a sting or an elephant a trunk. It is quite different if I say that the bee is busy or that the elephant is tremendously strong; this statement contains a certain recognition. I estimate the strength, but I do not estimate the trunk. There is the same element of estimation if I say that a man is sensible. But if I say that he is wise, why that's another matter; it is as if I said that I love him. In short, cleverness is a gift or talent; reason is a quality or strength, but wisdom is a virtue.

'And now I know what is the difference between these three words. Cleverness is usually cruel, malicious and selfish; it seeks the weakness in its neighbour and succeeds in exploiting it to its own profit; it leads to success.

'Reason is usually cruel to man but just to aims; it seeks the common gain; if it finds weakness or folly in a neighbour it seeks to remove it by advice or discipline; it leads to improvement.

'Wisdom cannot be cruel, for it is benevolence and sympathy; it does not seek the common gain, for it loves men too much to be able to love some more distant object; if it finds out the weakness or wretchedness of its neighbour it forgives it and loves it; it leads to harmony.

'Men of Boeotia, have you ever heard of the name "wise" being given to an unhappy man? or a buffoon? or an embittered and disappointed man? Consider why it is a custom even in unphilosophic life to call that man wise who cherishes the least hatred and who is on good terms with the world? Say the word "wisdom" over to yourselves again and again; say this word in joy or sorrow, say it when you are weary, angry and impatient; you will hear it in sorrow, but comforted, joy, but constantly and delicately repeated, weariness, but full of encouragement, patience and endless forgiveness; and all this, my friends, is the delightful and sorrowful sound, the voice in which wisdom speaks.

'Yes, wisdom is a kind of sadness. Man can put his whole reason into his work, he can realize it by his labours. But wisdom will always remain above every task. The wise man is like a gardener who is manuring a flower bed or fastening a rose to a stake and all the while may be thinking of God. His work does not contain or embody his wisdom. Reason is in action, but wisdom is in experience.

'But wise poets and artists are even able to embody this experience in their work; they do not give out their wisdom in actions but directly in experience. That is the especial value of art, and nothing in the world can compare with it.

'See, I have deviated altogether from my programme. But what more can I say? If wisdom lies in experience and not in ideas, it is unnecessary for me to read you my roll of parchment.'

(1920)

Alexander the Great

To Aristotle of Stagirus,
director of the school at Athens

My great and beloved teacher, dear Aristotle!

It is a very, very long time since I wrote to you; but as you know I have been over-occupied with military matters, and while we were marching through Hyrcania, Drangiana and Gedrosia, conquering Bactria and advancing beyond the Indus, I had neither the time nor the inclination to take up my pen. I have now been back in Susa for some months; but I have been so overwhelmed with administrative business, appointing officials and mopping up all kinds of intrigues and revolts that I have not had a moment till today to write to you about myself. Of course you know roughly from the official reports what I have been doing; but both my devotion to you and my confidence in your influence on cultivated Hellenic circles urge me once more to open my heart to you as my revered teacher and spiritual guide.

I remember that years ago (how far away it seems to me now!) I wrote you an absurd and enthusiastic letter on the tomb of Achilles; I was on the threshold of my Persian expedition and I vowed then that my model for life should be the valiant son of Peleus. I dreamed only of heroism and greatness; I had already won my victory over Thrace and I thought that I was advancing against Darius at the head of my Macedonians and Hellenes simply to cover myself with laurels worthy of my ancestors whom the divine Homer has sung. I can say that I did not fall short of my ideal either at Chaeronea or at Granicus; but today I hold a very different view of the political significance of my actions at that time. The sober truth is that our Macedonia, more or less united to Greece, was constantly threatened from the north by the Thracian barbarians; they could have attacked us at an unfavourable moment which the Greeks would have used to violate their treaty and break away from Macedonia. It was absolutely necessary to subdue Thrace so that Macedonia should have her flank covered in the event of Greek treachery. It was sheer political necessity, my dear Aristotle; but your pupil did not understand this thoroughly then and gave himself up to dreams of exploits like those of Achilles.

With the conquest of Thrace our situation changed: we controlled the whole of the western coast of the Ægean as far as the Bosphorus; but our mastery of the Ægean was threatened by the maritime power of Persia; bordering as we did on the Hellespont and the Bosphorus, we found ourselves in critical proximity to the Persian sphere of influence. Sooner or later there was bound to be a struggle between us and Persia over the Ægean Sea and the free passage of the Pontic Straits. Fortunately I struck before Darius was ready. I thought I was following in the footsteps of Achilles and should have the glory of conquering a new Ilium for Greece; actually, as I see today, it was absolutely necessary to drive the Persians back from the Ægean Sea; and I drove them back, my dear master, so thoroughly that I occupied the whole of Bithynia, Phrygia and Cappadocia, laid waste Cilicia and only stopped at Tarsus. Asia Minor was ours. Not only the old Ægean basin, but the whole northern coast of the Mediterranean or, as we call it, the Egyptian Sea, was in our hands.

You would have said, my dear Aristotle, that my principal political and strategic aim, namely the final expulsion of Persia from Hellenic waters, was now completely achieved. But with the conquest of Asia Minor a new situation arose : our new shores might be threatened from the south, that is from Phoenicia or Egypt; Persia might receive reinforcements or material from there for further wars against us. It was thus essential to occupy the Tyrian coasts and control Egypt; in this way we became masters of the entire littoral, but simultaneously a new danger arose : that Darius, relying on his rich Mesopotamia, might fling himself upon Syria, and tear our Egyptian dominions from our base in Asia Minor. I therefore had to crush Darius at any cost; I succeeded in doing this at Gaugamela; as you know, Babylon and Susa, Persepolis and Pasargadae dropped into our lap. This gave us control of the Persian Gulf; but so as to protect these new dominions against possible invasions from the north we had to set out northwards against the Medes and Hyrcanians. Now our dominions stretched from the Caspian Sea to the Persian Gulf, but lay open to the east; I advanced with my Macedonians to the borders of Area and Drangiana, I laid waste Gedrosia and gave Arachosia a thrashing, after which I occupied Bactria as a conqueror; and to safeguard these military victories by a lasting union, I took the Bactrian Princess Roxana to wife. It was a simple political necessity; I had conquered so many Eastern lands for my Macedonians and Greeks that willy-nilly I had to win over my barbarous Eastern subjects by my appearance and splendour, without which these poor shepherds cannot imagine a powerful ruler. The truth is that my old Macedonian Guard took it badly; perhaps they thought that their old commander was becoming estranged from his war comrades. Unfortunately I had to have my old friends Philotas and Calisthenes executed; my dear Parmenion lost his life too. I was very sorry about this; but it was unavoidable if the rebellion of my Macedonians was not to endanger my next step. I was, in fact, just preparing for my expedition to India. I must tell you that Gedrosia and Arachosia are enclosed within high mountains like fortifications; but for these fortifications to be impregnable they need a foreground from which to undertake a sally or a withdrawal behind the ramparts. This strategic foreground is India as far as the Indus. It was a military necessity to occupy this territory and with it the bridgehead on the further bank of the Indus; no responsible soldier or statesman would have acted otherwise; but when we reached the river Hyphasis my Macedonians began to make a fuss and say they were too tired, ill or homesick to go any further. I had to come back; it was a terrible journey for my veterans, but still worse for me; I had intended to reach the Bay of Bengal to secure a natural frontier in the east for my Macedonia, and now I was forced to abandon this task for a time.

I returned to Susa. I could be satisfied at having conquered such an empire for my Macedonians and Hellenes. But so as not to have to rely entirely on my exhausted people I took thirty thousand Persians into my army; they are good soldiers and I urgently need them for the defence of my Eastern frontiers. And do you know, my old soldiers are extremely annoyed about it. They cannot even understand that in winning for my people Oriental territories a hundred times greater than our own country I have become the great King of the East; that I must choose my officials and counsellors from amongst the Orientals and surround myself with an Oriental court; all this is a self-evident political necessity which I am carrying out in the interests of Greater Macedonia. Circumstances demand of me more and more personal sacrifices; I bear them without complaint, for I think of the greatness and strength of my beloved country. I have to endure the barbarous luxury of my power and magnificence; I have taken to wife three princesses of Eastern kingdoms; and now, my dear Aristotle, I have actually become a god.

Yes, my dear master, I have had myself proclaimed god; my good Eastern subjects kneel to me and bring me sacrifices. It is a political necessity if I am to have the requisite authority over these mountain shepherds and these camel drivers. How far away are the days when you taught me to use reason and logic! But reason itself bids me adapt my means to human unreason. At first glance my career must appear fantastic to anyone; but now when I think it over at night in the quiet of my godlike study I see that I have never undertaken anything which was not rendered absolutely necessary by my preceding step.

You see, my dear Aristotle, it would be in the interests of peace and order, and consistent with political interests if I were recognized as god in my Western territories as well. It would free my hands here in the east if my own Macedonia and Hellas accepted the political principle of my absolute authority; I could set out with a quiet heart to secure for my own land of Greece her natural frontiers on the coast of China. I should thus secure the power and safety of my Macedonia for all eternity. As you see, this is a sober and reasonable plan; I have long ceased to be the visionary who swore an oath on the tomb of Achilles. If I ask you now as my wise friend and guide to prepare the way by philosophy and to justify my proclamation as god in such a way as to be acceptable to my Greeks and Macedonians, I do so as a responsible politician and states-man; I leave it to you to consider whether you wish to undertake this task as a reasonable and patriotic work and one which is politically necessary.

Greetings, my dear Aristotle, from your
Alexander

(1937)

The Death of Archimedes

THE story of Archimedes did not happen quite in the way that it has been written; it is true that he was killed when the Romans conquered Syracuse, but it is not correct that a Roman soldier burst into his house to plunder it and that Archimedes, absorbed in drawing a geometrical figure, growled at him crossly: 'Don't spoil my circles!' For one thing, Archimedes was not an absent-minded professor who did not know what was going on around him; on the contrary, he was by nature a thorough soldier who invented engines of war for the Syracusans for the defence of the city; for another thing, the Roman soldier was not a drunken plunderer but the educated and ambitious staff centurion Lucius, who knew to whom he had the honour of speaking and had not come to plunder but saluted on the threshold and said: 'Greetings, Archimedes.'

Archimedes raised his eyes from the wax tablet on which he was in fact drawing something and said: 'What is it?'

'Archimedes,' said Lucius, 'we know that without your engines of war Syracuse wouldn't have held out for a month; as it is, we have had our hands full with it for two years. Don't imagine that we soldiers don't appreciate that. They're magnificent engines. My congratulations.'

Archimedes waved his hand. 'Please don't, they're really nothing. Just ordinary mechanisms for throwing projectiles – mere toys. From a scientific point of view they have no great importance.'

'But from a military one they have,' said Lucius. 'Listen, Archimedes, I have come to ask you to work with us.'

'With whom?'

'With us, the Romans. After all, you must know that Carthage is on the decline. What is the use of helping her? We shall soon have the Carthaginians on the run, you'll see. You'd better join us, all of you.'

'Why?' growled Archimedes. 'We Syracusans happen to be Greeks. Why should we join you?'

'Because you live in Sicily, and we need Sicily.'

'And why do you need it?'

'Because we want to be masters of the Mediterranean.'

'Aha,' said Archimedes, and stared reflectively at his tablet. 'And why do you want that?'

'Whoever is master of the Mediterranean,' said Lucius, 'is master of the world. That's clear enough.'

'And must you be masters of the world?'

'Yes. The mission of Rome is to become master of the world. And I can tell you, that's what Rome is going to be.'

'Possibly,' said Archimedes and erased something on his tablet. 'But I wouldn't advise it, Lucius. Listen, to be master of the world – some day that's going to give you an awful lot of defending to do. It's a pity, all the trouble you're going to have with it.'

'That doesn't matter; we shall be a great empire.'

'A great empire,' murmured Archimedes. 'If I draw a small circle or a large circle, it's still only a circle. There are still frontiers – you will never be without frontiers, Lucius. Do you think that a large circle is more perfect than a small circle? Do you think you are a greater geometrician if you draw a larger circle?'

'You Greeks are always juggling with arguments,' objected the centurion. 'We have another way of proving that we are right.'

'How?'

'By action. For instance, we have conquered your Syracuse. Ergo, Syracuse belongs to us. Is that a clear proof?'

'Yes,' said Archimedes and scratched his head with his stylo. 'Yes, you have conquered Syracuse; only it is not and never will be the same Syracuse as it was before. Why, it used to be a great and famous city; now it will never be great again. Poor Syracuse!'

'But Rome will be great. Rome has got to be stronger than anyone else in the whole world.'

'Why?'

'To keep up her position. The stronger we are, the more enemies we have. That is why we must be the strongest.'

'As for strength,' murmured Archimedes, 'I'm a bit of a physicist, Lucius, and I'll tell you something. Force absorbs itself.'

'What does that mean?'

'It's just a law, Lucius. Force which is active absorbs itself. The stronger you are, the more of your strength you use up that way; and one day a time will come –'

'What were you going to say?'

'Oh, nothing. I'm not a prophet, Lucius; I'm only a physicist. Force absorbs force. I know no more than that.'

'Listen, Archimedes, wouldn't you like to work with us? You have no idea what tremendous possibilities would open out for you in Rome. You would build the strongest war machines in the world –'

'Forgive me, Lucius; I'm an old man and I should like to work out one or two of my ideas. As you see, I am just drawing something here.'

'Archimedes, aren't you attracted by the idea of winning world mastery with us? – Why don't you answer?'

'I beg your pardon,' grunted Archimedes, bending over his tablets. 'What did you say?'

'That a man like you might win world mastery.'

'Hm, world mastery,' said Archimedes in a bored tone. 'You mustn't be offended, but I've something more important here. Something more lasting, you know. Something which will really endure.'

'What's that?'

'Mind! Don't spoil my circles! It's the method of calculating the area of a segment of a circle.'

*

Later it was reported that the learned Archimedes had lost his life through an accident.

(1938)

The Roman Legions

FOUR of Caesar's veterans, who had been through the campaigns in Gaul and Britain and had come back covered with glory and with the greatest triumph which the world had ever seen, these four heroes, Bullio, an ex-corporal, Lucius called Macer because of his thinness, Sartor called Hilla, a veteran of the Second Legion, and Strobus of Gaeta, met at the wine shop of Onocrates, a Greek from Sicily and a great wag, to talk over together the great and memorable military events which they had witnessed. As it was rather hot Onocrates set a table for them in the street, and there the four soldiers sat drinking, talking in loud voices. Who can wonder that the people in the street soon crowded round them, craftsmen, donkey drivers, children, and women with babies in their arms, to listen to what they said? I tell you, great Caesar's famous exploits still awakened the interest of all Roman citizens.

'Just you listen to what happened when we were drawn up beside that river with thirty thousand Senones facing us,' said Strobus of Gaeta.

'Half a mo',' Bullio pulled him up. 'For one thing there weren't thirty thousand of the Senones, but barely eighteen thousand, and for another, you were with the Ninth Legion, which never stood against the Senones. You were lying in camp in Aquitania and mending our boots for us, because the men serving with you were all cobblers and shoemakers. All right. Go on.'

'You're mixing it all up,' objected Strobus. 'Let me tell you: we were lying at Lutetia. And we mended your boots for you that time when you wore them right through running away from Gergovia. You got a jolly good hiding there, you and the Fifth Legion, and it served you right.'

'It wasn't like that at all,' said Lucius called Macer. 'The Fifth Legion was never at Gergovia. The Fifth Legion got a kick in the pants right away at Bibracta, and after that you couldn't get them anywhere except out scrounging. That was a nice legion for you,' said Macer, spitting a long way.

'And whose fault was it that the Fifth Legion got in the soup at Bibracta?' demanded Bullio. 'The Sixth was to have advanced to relieve them, but the Sixth didn't want to, the lazy blighters. They were fresh from the girls at Massilia –'

'You've got it wrong,' objected Sartor called Hilla. 'The Sixth Legion wasn't at Bibracta at all; it only came up to the front line at Axona, when Galba was in command.'

'A fat lot you know about it, you bastard,' retorted Bullio; 'at Axona there were the Second, Third and Seventh Legions. The Eburoni had sent the Sixth running back to their mammies long before that.'

'That's all a pack of lies,' said Lucius Macer. 'The only bit that's true is that the Second Legion, in which I served, fought at Axona; all the rest you made up.'

'Tell us another!' said Strobus of Gaeta. 'At Axona you were snoring in the reserve, and by the time you woke up the battle was over. To burn Cenabun, now, you could manage that, and to slaughter a couple of hundred civilians for hanging three moneylenders, you were brave enough for that too.'

'Caesar ordered it,' said Macer, shrugging his shoulders.

'That's not true!' shouted Hilla. 'It wasn't Caesar

ordered it, it was Labienus. Why, Caesar was too much of a politician for that; but Labienus was a soldier.'

'Galba was a soldier,' said Bullio, 'because he wasn't afraid; but Labienus always stuck half a mile behind the front line so that he shouldn't get hit. Where was Labienus when the Nervii surrounded us, eh? Our centurion fell then, and as senior corporal I took over the command. "Boys," I said, "anyone who yields an inch –"'

'That wasn't with the Nervii,' Strobus interrupted him; 'they shot at you with arrows and slings. But it was worse with the Arverni.'

'Tell that to the horse marines!' retorted Macer. 'We were never able to catch up with the Arverni at all. I tell you chaps, it was like trying to catch a hare!'

'In Aquitania,' said Hilla, 'I once shot a stag; he was a fellow, I tell you, he had antlers like a tree – two horses had to drag him into camp.'

'That's nothing,' declared Strobus. 'In Britain, now, there were deer for you!'

'Go on!' shouted Bullio. 'Here's Strobus making out he was in Britain!'

'You never went there either,' retorted Macer. 'Ho, Onocrates, wine! I tell you, I've met plenty of liars who said they'd been to Britain, but I never believed one of them.'

'I was there,' said Hilla. 'I hunted boars there. The Seventh, Eighth and Tenth Legions were there.'

'Don't talk nonsense, man,' said Strobus. 'The Tenth never went further than the camp of the Sequanes. You should have seen how smart they were when they arrived at Alesia. But they got their belly full there, the milksops.'

'We all got our belly full there,' said Bullio. 'We were thrashed like rye, but we won for all that.'

'That's all rot,' retorted Macer. 'It wasn't a big battle at all. When I crawled out of the tent at dawn –'

'Nonsense,' said Hilla. 'At Alesia it started in the night.'

'Go and boil yourself,' said Bullio; 'it began after dinner; we'd just had mutton –'

'That's a lie!' shouted Hilla, thumping the table. 'At Alesia we had beef because the cows went sick on us. No one would eat it.'

'I tell you it was mutton,' insisted Bullio. 'The centurion Longus had just come to us from the Fifth Legion –'

'Why, man, Longus was with us, the Second,' said Macer, 'and he was killed long before Alesia. Hirtus was with the Fifth.'

'He wasn't,' said Hilla. 'The Fifth had that fellow – what was his name? – yes, Corda.'

'Nonsense,' said Bullio. 'Corda was at Massilia. It was Longus, I tell you; he came and said "this blasted rain –".'

'Oh, shut up!' shouted Strobus. 'He didn't. It didn't rain at all at Alesia. It was frightfully hot. I remember how the pork stank.'

'It was mutton,' yelled Bullio, 'and it was raining! and then Hirtus came to us and said: "Boys, I think we're in for it!" And he was right. The battle lasted twenty hours –'

'It didn't,' said Macer. 'It was all over in three hours.'

'You've got it all mixed up,' said Strobus. 'It went on for three days, on and off. The second day we lost –'

'We didn't,' declared Hilla. 'We lost the first day, but the second day we won.'

'Rot,' said Bullio, 'we didn't win at all and we were just going to surrender, but they surrendered first.'

'It wasn't like that at all,' retorted Macer, 'anyway, there wasn't any battle at Alesia. Onocrates, wine! Just

you wait, I'll tell you something: when we were besieging
Avaricum –'

'Oh, can it !' grunted Bullio and went to sleep.

The Ten Righteous

And the Lord said, Because the cry of Sodom and Gomorrah is great, and because their sin is very grievous;

I will go down now, and see whether they have done altogether according to the cry of it, which is come unto me; and if not, I will know . . .

And Abraham drew near, and said, Wilt thou also destroy the righteous with the wicked?

Peradventure there be fifty righteous within the city: wilt thou also destroy and not spare the place for the fifty righteous that are therein? . . .

And the Lord said, If I find in Sodom fifty righteous within the city, then will I spare all the place for their sakes . . .

And Abraham answered and said . . . Peradventure there shall lack five of the fifty righteous: wilt thou destroy all the city for lack of five? And he said, If I find there forty and five, I will not destroy it.

And he spake unto him yet again, and said, Peradventure there shall be forty found there. And he said, I will not do it for forty's sake.

And he said unto him, Oh let not the Lord be angry, and I will speak: Peradventure there shall thirty be found there. And he said, I will not do it, if I find thirty there.

And he said, Behold now, I have taken upon me to speak unto the Lord: Peradventure there shall be twenty found there. And he said, I will not destroy it for twenty's sake.

And he said, Oh let not the Lord be angry, and I will speak yet but this once: Peradventure ten shall be found there. And he said, I will not destroy it for ten's sake.

And the Lord went his way, as soon as he had left communing with Abraham; and Abraham returned unto his place.

(Gen. xviii. 20–33)

AND when he had gone back to his own place, Abraham called his wife Sarah and said to her: 'Listen, I've heard this from the most reliable source, but nobody must know. The Lord has decided to destroy Sodom and Gomorrah because of their sins. He told me so himself.'

And Sarah said: 'There now, isn't that what I've said all along? And when I told you about the goings on there you stood up for them and hushed me up and said, "Be quiet. Don't put your word in. What is it to do with you?" Now you see, I told you what would happen. Once when I was talking about it to Lot's wife, I said to her: "What's going to come of all this?" Do you think the Lord will destroy Lot's wife, too?'

Abraham answered and said: 'That's just the point. You see, under pressure from me the Lord consented to spare Sodom and Gomorrah if He found fifty righteous there. But I managed to get the number down to ten. That's why I called you, so that we can choose ten righteous for the Lord.'

Sarah said: 'That's a good thing. Lot's wife is a friend of mine, and Lot is the son of your brother Haran. I don't say Lot is righteous. You know how he incited all his house against you – you needn't tell me, Abraham, that there wasn't something fishy about that. He doesn't mean rightly by you, but he is your nephew, even if Haran hasn't behaved to you as a blood brother should; still, he's one of the family.'

And she spoke further, saying: 'Tell the Lord to spare Gomorrah. I'm sure I don't wish anybody any harm. I'm like that. My legs shake under me at the thought of so many people losing their lives. Go and intercede with the Lord to have mercy on them.'

Then Abraham answered: 'The Lord will have mercy if he finds ten righteous. I think we might tell Him which they are. Run over the names of all the people who live in Sodom and Gomorrah. There's no reason why we shouldn't help the Lord to find ten righteous.'

And Sarah said: 'Nothing's easier. I'll soon find Him twenty, or fifty, or even a hundred righteous. There's Lot's wife and Lot, your nephew; it's true he is treacherous and envious, still he's one of the family. That's two already.'

On that Abraham said: 'And their two daughters.'

Then said Sarah: 'What are you thinking of, Abraham? The older one, Jesha, is a hussy. Haven't you noticed how she swings her hips as she passes you? Lot's wife said to me herself: I'm very worried about Jesha, I shall be glad when she's married. The younger girl looks to me better behaved. But if you think we should, then count them both in.'

Abraham said: 'So we've got four righteous already. Whom else shall we choose?'

And Sarah answered: 'If you count those two girls, you must include the young men they are promised to, Jobab and Seboim.'

But Abraham said: 'What talk is this? Seboim is the son of old Dodanim. Can the son of an evil-doer and a usurer be righteous?'

And Sarah said: 'Abraham, do it, please, please do, for the sake of the family. Why should not Melcha be promised to as good a man as that hussy of a Jesha? She's a good girl and at least she doesn't swing her bottom at her elderly relations whom she ought to respect.'

Abraham answered: 'It shall be as you say. So now with Jobab and Seboim we've got six righteous. We only need to find four more.'

And Sarah said: 'That'll be easy. Let's see, who else in Sodom is righteous?'

Then Abraham said: 'I should say old Nachor was.'

But Sarah said: 'I'm surprised that you can speak his name at all. Doesn't he sleep with heathen women, old though he is? I should say Sabatach was more righteous than Nachor.'

Then Abraham broke out in anger and said: 'Sabatach is a perjurer. Don't ask me to give his name to the Lord among the righteous. Elmodad or Eliab would be a better choice.'

On that Sarah said: 'Then let me tell you, Eliab committed adultery with Elmodad's wife. If Elmodad were worth anything, he'd throw that slut of a wife of his into the street, where she belongs. But perhaps you might suggest Naaman; he isn't responsible for what he does, because he's crazy.'

And Abraham answered: 'I shall not suggest Naaman; I'll suggest Melchiel.'

And Sarah said: 'If you do, I'll never speak to you again. Wasn't it Melchiel who made mock of you because you have had no son by me but only by that girl Hagar?'

Then Abraham said: 'I will not give the name of Melchiel. Do you think I'd better count Ezron or Jahelel among the righteous?'

Sarah answered and said: 'Jahelel is a glutton and Ezron carries on with the harlots of Achad.'

And Abraham said: 'I will speak for Ephraim.'

But Sarah said: 'Ephraim says that the vale of Mamre, where our flocks are pastured, belongs to him.'

Then Abraham said: 'Ephraim is not a righteous man. I will speak for Ahiram, the son of Jasiel.'

And Sarah said: 'Ahiram is the friend of Melchiel. If you want to speak for anyone, speak for Nadab.'

Abraham answered: 'Nadab is a miser. I will speak for Amram.'

Sarah said: 'Amram wanted to sleep with your girl Hagar. I'm sure I don't know what he saw in her. Asriel is a better man.'

But Abraham said: 'Asriel is a coxcomb. I cannot suggest a buffoon to the Lord. Supposing I named Namuel? No, even Namuel doesn't deserve it. Why should it be Namuel of all people?'

Then Sarah said: 'What have you against Namuel? He's stupid but he's pious.'

And Abraham said: 'So be it. Namuel is the seventh.'

Upon that Sarah said: 'Wait, Namuel won't do, for he practises the sin of Sodom. Who else is there in Sodom? Let me say them over: Kalhat, Salfad, Itamar . . .'

Abraham answered: 'Put that idea out of your head. Itamar is a liar, and as for Kalhat and Salfad, don't they both take the side of the accursed Peleg? But perhaps you know some righteous woman in Sodom. Do try and think.'

And Sarah said: 'There is not one.'

Then Abraham lamented and said: 'What, are there not ten righteous men in Sodom and Gomorrah that the Lord may spare those fair cities for their sakes?'

Sarah said: 'Go, Abraham, go to the Lord again, fall on your knees before His face, rend your garments and say, Lord, Lord, I and Sarah my wife beseech you with tears not to destroy Sodom and Gomorrah for their sins.

'And say to Him: Have mercy on those sinful people and spare them. Have mercy, Lord, and let them live. Do not ask it of us, Lord, that we should give you the names of ten righteous men from among all Thy people.'

Pseudo Lot, or Concerning Patriotism

And there came two angels to Sodom at even, and Lot sat in the gate of Sodom. And Lot seeing them rose up to meet them; and he bowed himself with his face toward the ground.

And he said, Behold now, my lords, turn in, I pray you, into your servant's house, and tarry all night, and wash your feet, and you shall rise up early and go on your ways. And they said, Nay, we will abide in the street all night.

And he pressed upon them greatly, and they turned in unto him and entered into his house; and he made them a feast, and did bake unleavened bread, and they did eat.

And the men said unto Lot: Hast thou here any besides? son-in-law, and thy sons, and thy daughters, and whatsoever thou has in the city, bring them out of this place;

For we will destroy this place, because the cry of them is waxen great before the face of the Lord; and the Lord hath sent us to destroy it.

LOT was amazed when he heard this and said: 'And why am I to go away from here?' But they said to him: 'Because the Lord does not wish to destroy the righteous.'

Lot was silent for a long time, but at last he said: 'I pray you, sirs, let me go forth and tell my sons-in-law and my daughters to make ready for the journey.' They answered him: 'Do so.'

And Lot went out; he hurried through the streets of the city and cried to all the people: 'Up, get you out of this

*place: for the Lord will destroy this city.' But he seemed
unto them as one that mocked.*

Lot returned home, but he did not lie down, but pondered the whole night long.

*And when the morning arose, then the angels hastened
Lot, saying, Arise, take thy wife, and thy two daughters,
which are here; lest thou be consumed in the iniquity of
the city.*

'I am not coming,' said Lot. 'Forgive me, but I am not
coming. I have thought about it all night. I cannot go
away, for I am one of the people of Sodom.'

'You are righteous,' objected the angels, 'but they are
unrighteous and the cry of them is waxen great before the
face of the Lord. What have you to do with them?'

'I don't know,' said Lot. 'I have been thinking about that
too, about what I have to do with them; all my life I have
complained of my fellow countrymen and I have judged
them so severely that it is terrible for me to remember it
now: for they are to be destroyed. And when I went to
the city of Segor it seemed to me that its people were
better than the people of Sodom.'

'Up,' said the angels, 'you shall go to the city of Segor;
for it will be saved.'

'What is Segor to me?' answered Lot. 'There is one
righteous man in Segor: whenever I talked with him he
complained of his fellow citizens, and I cursed the people
of Sodom for their sins, but now I cannot go away. I pray
you, leave me.'

And the angel spoke and said: 'The Lord has commanded that the people of Sodom be destroyed.'

'His will be done,' said Lot quietly. 'I have thought
about it all night; and I remembered so many things that I
wept. Have you ever heard the people of Sodom sing? No,
you do not know them at all, for then you would not have

come like this. When the girls walk along the streets they swing their hips and hum a tune between their lips; and they laugh as they draw water in their pitchers. No water is clearer than that from the springs of Sodom; and no tongue of all the tongues has a fairer sound. When a child speaks I understand him as if he were my own; and when they play, they play the same games that I played when I was little. And when I cried, my mother comforted me in the speech of Sodom. Oh Lord!' Lot cried aloud, 'as if it were yesterday!'

'The people of Sodom have sinned,' said the second angel severely, 'and therefore –'

'They have sinned, I know,' Lot interrupted him impatiently. 'But have you seen our craftsmen? They look as if they were playing a game; and when they make a pitcher or a shirt your heart leaps for joy, it is so beautifully done. They are such deft craftsmen that you could watch them all day long; and when you see them committing these dreadful sins it grieves you more than if a man of Segor did it. It torments you as if you had a share in their guilt. What use is my righteousness to me if I belong to Sodom? If you condemn Sodom, you condemn me. I am not righteous. I am like them. I will not go away from here.'

'You will be destroyed with them,' said the angel frowning.

'Perhaps; but first I shall try to keep them from being destroyed. I don't know what I shall do; but to the very last minute I shall think I must help them. How can I just go off? I am resisting the Lord and so He will not hear me. If He would give me three years, or three days, or at least three hours! What difference would three hours make to Him? If yesterday He had commanded me: Go forth from their midst, for they are unrighteous, I should have said to Him : Have patience yet a little, I will speak a word to one and another; I have condemned them instead of going amongst them. But how can I leave them now, when they are to be destroyed? Is it not partly my fault that things have gone so far? I don't want to die; but I can't bear that they should die either. I shall stay.'

'You will not save Sodom.'

'I know I shan't; what could I do? But I shall try to do something, I don't know what yet; I only know I must stay. Because all my life I have judged them more harshly than anyone else; because I have borne their heaviest burden with them : their faults. Lord, I do not know how to say what they are to me; I can only show it by staying with them.'

'Your people,' said the angel, 'are those who are righteous and believe in the same God as you; but the sinful, the godless and the idolaters are not your people.'

'How can they fail to be, when they are the people of Sodom? You don't understand, because you do not know the voice of flesh and clay. What is Sodom? You say it is a city of unrighteousness. But when the people of Sodom fight, they do not fight for their unrighteousness but for something better which was or will be; and even the worst of them may fall for the sake of all. Sodom means all of us; and if I have any merit in the eyes of the Lord, let him account it to Sodom and not to me. What more shall I say? Tell the Lord: Lot, Thy servant, will place himself before the men of Sodom and will defend them against Thee as if Thou wert his enemy.'

'Hold your peace !' cried the angel. 'Your sin is terrible; but the Lord has not heard you. Make ready and come forth from this city : save at least your wife and the two daughters whom you have.'

Then Lot wept: 'Yes, I must save them, you are right. I pray you, lead me.'

And while he lingered, the angels laid hold upon his hand, and upon the hand of his wife, and upon the hand of his two daughters: the Lord being merciful unto him.

(While they were leading him forth Lot prayed, saying:)

'Everything which life gave me it gave me by thy hands; it made my flesh of thy clay and put in my mouth the words which are in the mouths of thy men and women; and therefore I loved them with each of my words, even when I cursed them.'

'I see thee even when I close my eyes, for thou art deeper than my sight; thou art in me, even as I have been in thee.'

'My hands perform thy customs unwittingly; and if I were in the desert, my feet would walk in the direction of thy streets.'

'Sodom, Sodom, art thou not the fairest of cities? And if I saw only a little window, curtained with striped linen, I should know: that is one of the windows of Sodom.'

'I am like a dog whom they lead from the house of his master; even if he droops his muzzle in the dust so as not to see, he still knows the smell of the familiar things.'

'I believed in the Lord and His law; I did not believe in thee, but thou art; and other lands are as a shadow through which I pass, nor can I lean against a wall or a tree; they are like a shadow.'

'But thou art as nothing else: and everything that is, is only in comparison with thee. If I look upon thee I see only thee, and if I look upon something else, I see it only as compared with thee.'

'I believed in the Lord because it seemed to me that He was the God of Sodom; if there is no Sodom, there is no God.'

'Oh gates, gates of Sodom, where are they leading me and into what emptiness? Where shall I set my foot? for there is no earth beneath me and I stand as one that stands not. Go, my daughters, and leave me; I can go no further.'

And they brought him forth and set him without the city: and there they spake unto him saying: Escape for thy life; look not behind thee, neither stay thou in all the plain, lest thou be consumed.

The sun was risen upon the earth when they said this.

Then the Lord rained upon Sodom and upon Gomorrah brimstone and fire from the Lord out of heaven.

Then Lot looked round and gave a great cry and hastened back towards the city.

'What are you doing, accursed one?' the angels called after him.

'I am going to help the people of Sodom,' answered Lot, and went into the city.

(1923)

Christmas Eve

'WELL, I'm surprised at you!' cried Mistress Dinah. 'If they'd been decent folk they'd have gone to the mayor instead of begging their way like this! Why didn't you send them to Simon's house? Why on earth must we be the ones to take them in? Aren't we as good as Simon? I know his wife would never let riff-raff like that into her house! I'm surprised at you, I really am, for demeaning yourself to have anything to do with such people!'

'Don't shout so,' grunted old Isachar, 'they'll hear what you say.'

'Let them hear!' shouted Mistress Dinah, raising her voice still more. 'What next! It's a nice look-out if I'm not even to whisper in my own house because of tramps like that! Do you know them? Does anybody know them? He says she's his wife. His wife, is she? I know the sort of thing that goes on among those vagrants. Aren't you ashamed to let such people into the house?'

Isachar wanted to point out that he had only let them into the cow-house, but he kept it to himself; he liked a quiet life.

'And that woman,' Mistress Dinah went on indignantly, 'it's obvious what her condition is. My God, as if things weren't bad enough without that! Just think of all the gossip there will be! What can you have been thinking of?' Mistress Dinah paused for breath. 'Of course, you can't say no to a young thing like that. She's only to look sweet at you and you can't do enough for her. You wouldn't have done as much for *me*, Isachar! Just make yourselves comfortable, good people, there's lots of straw in the cow-house... As though we were the only people in all Bethlehem who have a cow-house! Why didn't Simon give them a truss of straw? Because his wife wouldn't put up with such behaviour from her husband, do you understand? It's only I who am such a poor, downtrodden wife that I put up with it all without a murmur.'

Old Isachar turned to the wall. 'Will she ever stop?' he thought. 'She's partly right, but to make such a fuss about a poor –'

'Bringing strangers into the house!' went on Mistress Dinah in righteous wrath. 'Who knows what sort of people they are? Now I shan't close an eye all night long for fright! But a lot you care whether I do or not! Everything for strangers, nothing for me! You might just once have a little consideration for your overworked and ailing wife! And in the morning I shall have to clear up after them! If the fellow really is a carpenter, why hasn't he got a job? And why must I be the one to have all this trouble? Are you listening, Isachar?'

But Isachar, with his face to the wall, pretended to be asleep.

'Heavens,' sighed Dinah, 'what a life I have of it! I shall be awake all night now worrying... And there he sleeps like a log! They might carry off the whole house while he's snoring away... My God, the worries I have!'

And there was silence. Only old Isachar's regular snoring cleft the night at intervals.

*

Towards midnight he was waked out of a doze by a woman's stifled moans. 'Damn it,' he thought in alarm, 'that was in the cow-house next door ! I only hope it won't wake Dinah . . . She'll start creating again !'

And he lay without moving, as if he were asleep.

A moment later there was another moan. 'God, be merciful ! Oh God, grant that Dinah doesn't wake up,' prayed old Isachar in anguish, but just then he felt Dinah stir beside him, raise herself and listen in strained attention. 'It'll be awful,' thought Isachar in dismay, but he lay low and said nothing.

Mistress Dinah got up without a word, flung a rug round her and went out into the yard. 'Maybe she'll throw them out,' thought Isachar helplessly. 'I'm not going to be mixed up in it. She can do what she likes . . .'

After a strangely long and whispering moment, Dinah came back treading carefully. Drowsily, Isachar thought he heard the snap and crackle of wood, but he decided not to move. Perhaps Dinah felt cold, he thought, and was lighting a fire.

Then Dinah slipped away again quietly. Isachar half-opened his eyes and saw a kettle of water over the blazing fire. Whatever's that for? he thought in astonishment, and fell asleep again at once. He did not wake till Dinah went hurrying out into the yard with queer, eager, important little steps, carrying the steaming kettle.

Isachar was very puzzled. He got up and put on a few clothes. I must see what's going on, he said to himself energetically, but in the doorway he ran into Dinah.

'Gracious, what a hurry you're in !' he wanted to snap at her, but he had no time.

'What are you standing there gaping for?' she burst out at him, and hurried into the yard again with her arms full of scraps of stuff and strips of linen. She turned on the threshold. 'Go back to bed,' she cried harshly, 'and . . .

and don't come bothering us and getting in the way, d'you hear?'

Old Isachar strolled out into the yard. In front of the cow-house he saw the broad-shouldered form of a man hanging about, and went towards him. 'Well, well,' he grunted soothingly, 'turned you out, has she? Women, you know, Joseph . . .' And to divert the conversation from men's helplessness he pointed suddenly: 'Look, a star! Did you ever see such a star!'

Martha and Mary

Now it came to pass, as they went, that he entered into a certain village: and a certain woman named Martha received him into her house.

And she had a sister called Mary, which also sat at Jesus' feet, and heard his word.

But Martha was cumbered about much serving, and came to him, and said, Lord, dost thou not care that my sister hath left me to serve alone? bid her therefore that she help me.

And Jesus answered and said unto her, Martha, Martha, thou art careful and troubled about many things:

But one thing is needful: and Mary hath chosen that good part, which shall not be taken away from her.

(Luke x. 38–42)

BUT that evening Martha dropped in to see her neighbour Tamar, Jacob Grünfeld's wife, who lay in childbed; and seeing that the fire on the hearth was going out, she fetched logs and sat down beside the hearth to tend the fire. And when the flames sprang up, Martha stared into the fire and was silent.

Then Tamar said: 'You're so good, Martha. You think of everything. I don't know how I can ever repay you.'

But Martha said nothing and did not even turn her eyes away from the fire.

Then Tamar asked: 'Is it true, Martha dear, that the Rabbi from Nazareth came to your house today?'

And Martha answered: 'He came.'

Tamar clasped her hands and said: 'How happy that

must have made you, Martha. I knew He wouldn't come to us, but you deserve it, you're such a good housewife –'

Martha bent over the fire, straightened the logs with a jerk and said: 'To tell you the truth, Tamar, I can't abide the sight of myself. If I'd had any idea that today of all days – on the eve of the festival – Well, I thought to myself, I'll get the washing done early. You know our Mary and what a lot of washing she makes. So I was throwing all the dirty clothes together in a heap, and all at once "Good morrow, daughter," and He was standing in the doorway. I began calling "Mary! Mary! come here!" for her to help me clear away the heap of linen – Mary came running with her hair all loose, and the moment she sees Him she begins to scream like a mad thing: "Master, you have come to us?" and plump, down she goes on her knees before Him, sobbing and kissing his hands. I was so ashamed of her. What must the Master think of her, the crazy, hysterical girl, and all the dirty clothes all over the place? I just managed to blurt out: "Master, pray be seated," and grabbed the washing together. And Mary was holding on to his hand and sobbing: "Master, speak, speak to us, Rabboni!" – just think, Tamar, she called him Rabboni! And the whole place so untidy – you know what it's like on washing-day, I hadn't even swept the rooms – I can't think what He must have thought of us!'

'Never mind, Martha dear,' Mrs Grünfeld tried to comfort her. 'Men don't notice as a rule when things are a bit untidy like that. I know them.'

'That's as may be,' pronounced Martha with a hard gleam in her eye. 'Things *ought to* be clean and tidy. You know that time when the Master was at dinner at the Pharisee's house and our Mary washed His feet with her tears and dried them with her hair – I must say I'd never have been so forward as to do a thing like that myself, but

I would at least have liked to give Him a clean floor under
His feet. Yes, indeed. And to spread that nice rug before
Him, you know, the one from Damascus. Not dirty washing! Wiping His feet with tears and hair is all very well
for our Mary, but will she do her hair tidily when He
comes to see us? Not a bit of it! And wipe the floor for
Him? Not she! Just sitting there on the ground before
Him, with her eyes as big as saucers and saying, "Talk to
us, Rabboni!"'

'And did He talk?' asked Tamar eagerly.

'He talked,' said Martha slowly. 'He smiled and talked
to Mary. You know, what with first having the dirty
clothes to clear up and then getting Him at least a drink
of goat's milk and a piece of bread – He looked worn out.
It was on the tip of my tongue to say, "Master, I'll bring
some cushions, do have a nice rest – just forty winks –
and we'll be as quiet as mice, not make a sound –" but you
know, Tamar, one doesn't like to break in on what He's
saying. So I walked on tiptoe to give Mary the hint to be
quiet, but not a bit of it. "Go on talking, Master, please,
please tell us more!" and kind-hearted as He is, He smiled
and went on talking –'

'Oh, how I should have loved to hear what He said!'
sighed Tamar.

'So should I,' said Martha drily. 'But someone had to
cool the milk for Him, to keep it fresh. And someone had
to get a little honey from somewhere for His bread. Then I
had to run across to Ephraim's – I'd promised his wife to
keep an eye on the children while she went to market –
you know, Tamar, even an old maid like me can be useful
in her way. If only our brother Lazarus had been at home!
But early this morning, when Lazarus saw it was washing
day, he said: "Bye bye, girls, I'm off. But Martha, keep

a look out, and if that seed merchant from Lebanon comes along, buy me some of that tea for the lungs," – you know, our Lazarus has a delicate chest, Tamar, and he's getting worse. So I kept on thinking, if Lazarus came back while the Master was here – d'you know, I believe He could cure our Lazarus ! So every time I heard footsteps I flew out of the house and kept on calling to whoever I saw : "Mr Asher, Mr Levi, Mr Isachar, if you meet my brother Lazarus, do tell him to come home at once !" And I had to keep a look out for the seed merchant too – I simply didn't know which way to turn.'

'I know how it is,' said Mrs Grünfeld. 'A family gives one a lot of worry.'

'It isn't the worry I mind,' said Martha. 'But you know, Tamar, one would like to listen to the Word of God as well. I know I'm only a foolish woman, just a drudge – but I say to myself, someone must do it, someone must cook and wash and mend and keep the place clean, and our Mary hasn't the gift that way. She's going off in her looks now, Tamar; but she used to be such a lovely girl that I – I – I simply *had* to do things for her, d'you see what I mean? And all the while people think I'm ill-tempered. Now I ask you, Tamar, you know about these things, can an ill-tempered and unhappy woman cook well? And I'm not a bad cook. If Mary's so lovely, let her do the cooking, that's what I say. But, Tamar, I dare say you know how it is : sometimes you fold your hands in your lap, just for a minute or two, and then such queer thoughts come into your head. You feel that someone will say something to you or look at you somehow ... as if they were saying : Daughter, you clothe us with your love, you give us the whole of yourself, you sweep with your body and keep everything clean with the cleanliness of your spirit; we come into your house as if it were you yourself. Martha, you too have in your own way loved much –'

'Yes, that's how it is,' said Mrs Grünfeld. 'And if you'd had six children like me, you'd know it.'

Then Martha said : 'Tamar, when He came so suddenly, the Master from Nazareth, I was almost afraid that perhaps – perhaps He had come to say the lovely things to me that I've been waiting all these years to hear – and then for everything to be in such a mess! I had such a lump in my throat, I couldn't speak . . . I said to myself, it'll pass, I'm a foolish woman, in the meantime I'll put the washing to soak and run across to Ephraim's and send for our Lazarus and drive the fowls out of the yard, so that they don't disturb Him . . . And then when everything was done I was filled with such a beautiful certainty that now I was all ready to hear the Word of God. So I slipped quietly into the room where He sat talking. Mary was sitting at his feet, she didn't take her eyes off Him –' Martha smiled drily. 'I wondered how I should look if I stared at Him like that! And, Tamar, He looked at me with such clear and kindly eyes, as if He were going to say something. And all of a sudden it came over me – oh dear, how thin He is! You know, He never has a square meal, He hardly even touched the bread and honey – And then I thought: Pigeons! I'll roast Him a brace of pigeons! I'll send Mary to the market for them while He rests for a little – "Mary," I said, "come into the kitchen for a minute." But Mary took no notice, she might have been blind and deaf.'

'She didn't want to leave her guest alone,' said Tamar soothingly.

'She might have taken the trouble to see He had something to eat!' said Martha in a hard voice. 'That's what we women are for, isn't it? And when I saw that Mary took no notice but just stared as if she were in a trance, I – Tamar, I don't know how it happened, but I had to say it. And I said "Lord, is it nothing to you that my sister leaves me to do all the work alone? Tell her to help me in the kitchen!" I just burst out with it –'

'And did He tell her?' asked Mrs Grünfeld.

The tears burst from Martha's red eyes. '"Martha, Martha, you are careful and troubled about many things; but one thing is needful. Mary has chosen the better part, and it will never be taken away from her." That's what He said, Tamar, or something like it.'

There was a moment's silence. 'And was that all He said?' asked Tamar.

'All that I know of,' said Martha, wiping away her tears roughly. 'Then I went out and bought a brace of pigeons – such robbers as they are at the market, Tamar – and I roasted them and made you that drop of giblet soup –'

'It was good of you,' said Mrs Grünfeld. 'You are very good, Martha dear.'

'I'm not,' growled Martha. 'To tell you the truth, it's the first time my pigeons have ever been underdone. They were tough. But I – somehow I couldn't keep my mind on things. And I do believe in Him so tremendously, Tamar!'

'So do I,' said Tamar piously. 'And what else did He say, Martha? What did He say to Mary? What did He teach?'

'I don't know,' said Martha. 'I asked Mary, but you know how tiresome she is. "I don't know," she said, "honestly I couldn't repeat a word of it, to get it right, but it was all so marvellously beautiful, Martha, and I'm so frightfully happy –"'

'Well, that's something,' admitted Tamar.

Martha swallowed her tears, blew her nose noisily and said:

'There, give me the baby, Tamar, I'll change him for you.'

Lazarus

To Bethany came the news that the Galilean had been taken and cast into prison.

When Martha heard this she clasped her hands and the tears streamed from her eyes. 'There now!' she cried, 'I said so all along! Why did He go to Jerusalem? Why didn't He stay here? No one would have known about Him here. He could have gone on quietly with His carpentering – He could have set up his workshop here in our backyard ...'

Lazarus was pale and his eyes shone with emotion. 'That's a silly way to talk, Martha,' he said. 'He *had* to go to Jerusalem. He *had* to stand up among all those ... Pharisees and publicans, He *had* to tell them the truth to their faces. You women don't understand these things.'

'*I* understand,' said Mary quietly, with a rapt look. 'And let me tell you this: I *know* what's going to happen. There'll be a miracle. He will make a sign with His finger, and the walls of the prison will open, and everyone will know Him for what He is. They will fall on their knees before Him and cry "a miracle!" '

'Just you wait,' said Martha drily. 'He never could look after Himself. He won't do anything for Himself, won't raise a finger to save Himself, unless –' she added, wide-eyed, '– unless others help Him. Maybe He's waiting for them to come and help Him – all those who heard His words – all those whom He helped – for them to gird themselves up and hasten to Him –'

'I expect so,' remarked Lazarus. 'Never fear, girls, he has the whole of Judea behind Him. It would be a poor look out if – I say, I'd like to go and see it – Martha, get my things ready. I'm going to Jerusalem.'

Mary rose. 'I'm going too. To see the walls of the prison open and Him appear in heavenly glory – Martha, it will be simply marvellous !'

It was on the tip of Martha's tongue to say something, but she swallowed it down. 'Go along then, my dears,' she said. 'Somebody must stay here – to feed the chickens and the goats – I'll have your clothes ready in a minute and bake you a couple of cakes. I'm so glad you'll be there !'

*

When she came back with her face red from the glow of the oven, Lazarus was very pale and ill at ease. 'I don't feel well, Martha,' he said. 'What is it like out of doors?'

'Lovely and warm,' said Martha. 'You'll have pleasant walking.'

'It may be warm down here,' objected Lazarus. 'But up in Jerusalem there's always such a bitter wind.'

'I've put out your warm cloak for you,' said Martha.

'A warm cloak,' grumbled Lazarus, dissatisfied. 'It throws you into a sweat and then you get chilled, and there you are ! Feel, haven't I got a temperature? You know, I don't want to get ill on the journey – Mary wouldn't be a bit of use. And how could I help Him if I were ill?'

'You haven't got a temperature,' said Martha soothingly and thought to herself : 'My goodness, Lazarus is so queer ever since that time when he was raised from the dead.'

'*That time* it was the cold wind that got me, that time when – when I was so ill,' said Lazarus uneasily, for he did not care to remember his former death. 'You know, Martha dear, I've never felt quite myself since. I don't feel up to all this – the journey, the excitement. But of course I'll go, if only this shivering fit of mine will pass.'

'Of course you'll go,' said Martha with a heavy heart. 'Someone *must* go to His help. After all, He – cured you, didn't He?' she added uncertainly, for it seemed to her rather tactless to talk about his raising from the dead. 'Just think, Lazarus, when you've freed Him, you'll be able to ask Him to help you – if you don't happen to be feeling well.'

'That's true,' sighed Lazarus. 'But suppose I don't get so far? Or suppose we get there too late? You must think of all the things that may happen. And supposing there are riots in Jerusalem? You don't know these Roman soldiers, my girl. Oh dear, if only I were well !'

'Why, you *are* well, Lazarus,' said Martha. 'You *must* be well since He cured you.'

'Well !' said Lazarus bitterly. 'I'm the best person to know whether I'm well or not. I can only tell you that *since* that time I haven't felt really comfortable for a single moment. Not that I'm not awfully grateful to Him for – putting me on my feet again; you mustn't think that, Martha. But when you've known it as I have, that – that –' He shuddered and covered his face. 'Please, Martha, leave me now. I shall be better soon – I only need a minute – it's sure to pass.'

Martha sat down quietly in the yard; she stared in front of her with dry, unwinking eyes; her hands were clasped, but she was not praying. The black hens stood still to look at her with one eye; when, contrary to their expectations, she did not throw them any grain, they went to doze in the midday shade.

Lazarus slipped quietly out of the passage. He was

deathly pale and his teeth chattered. 'I – I can't now, Martha,' he stammered. 'And I did so want to go – perhaps tomorrow.'

There was a lump in Martha's throat. 'You'd better go and lie down, Lazarus,' she managed to say. 'You ... can't go.'

'I did want to go,' stammered Lazarus, 'but if you think, Martha ... Perhaps tomorrow ... But don't leave me at home alone, will you? What should I do all alone here?'

Martha got up. 'Just you go and lie down,' she said in her usual harsh voice. 'I'll stay with you.'

Just then Mary came out into the yard all ready for the journey. 'Now, Lazarus, shall we start?'

'Lazarus can't go,' said Martha drily. 'He isn't well.'

'Then I'll go alone,' sighed Mary, 'to see the miracle.'

The tears slowly trickled out of Lazarus's eyes. 'I should so much have liked to go too, Martha ... If I weren't so afraid ... of dying again!'

The Five Loaves

... WHAT have I against him? I'll tell you plainly, neighbour; it's not that I have anything against his teaching. Not at all. I once heard him preach, and I tell you, I was within an inch of becoming one of his disciples myself. Why, I went home and said to my cousin the harnessmaker: listen, you ought to hear him; I tell you, he's a prophet in his way. He says beautiful things and only what's true; your heart turns right over inside you; why, my eyes filled with tears and I'd have liked nothing better than to shut up my shop and follow him so as never to let him out of my sight. Give away all you have, he said, and follow me. Love your neighbour, help the poor and forgive those who wrong you, and things like that. I'm just an ordinary baker, but when I listened to him there was such a strange joy and pain within me, I don't know how to describe it: a kind of weight, so that I could have sunk to the ground and wept, and at the same time I felt lovely and light as though everything had dropped from my shoulders, you know, all my worries and trials. So I said to my cousin, you blockhead, you ought to be ashamed of yourself; you never talk anything but low, money-grubbing gossip about how much people owe you and how you have to pay tithes and taxes and interest; you should give everything you have to the poor, leave your wife and children, and follow him –

And as for curing the sick and those possessed, I don't hold that against him either. It's true it's a strange and unnatural power, but after all everyone knows our own doctors are quacks and the Roman ones aren't any better; they take your money all right, but when you call them in to a dying man they just shrug their shoulders and say you should have sent for them sooner. Sooner! My poor wife was ill for two years with haemorrhage before she died; I took her from doctor to doctor, you've no idea the money it cost, and none of them did her a bit of good. If he had been going from city to city then, I would have fallen on my knees before him and said: Lord, heal this woman! And she would have touched his garment and been healed. The poor thing suffered so, I can't tell you – So I approve of his healing the sick. You know the doctors cry out against it and say it's all fraud and trickery, and they would have liked to forbid him to do it and I don't know what; but of course there are all sorts of interests involved. The man who wants to help the people and save the world always comes up against somebody's interests; you can't please everyone, it isn't possible. I say let him heal them, and maybe even raise the dead; but that business with the five loaves was a thing he shouldn't have done. Speaking as a baker I tell you it was a great injustice to bakers.

You haven't heard about the affair of the five loaves? I'm surprised at that; all the bakers are quite beside themselves about it. Well, it's said that a great multitude followed him to a desert place and he healed their sick. And when it was evening his disciples came to him, saying: 'This is a desert place and the time is now past. Send the multitude away, that they may go into the villages and buy themselves victuals.' But he said to them: 'They need not depart, give ye them to eat.' And they say unto him: 'We have here but five loaves and two fishes.' He said: 'Bring them hither to me.' And he commanded the multitude to sit down on the grass, and took the five loaves and the two fishes, and looking up to heaven he blessed and brake and gave the loaves to his disciples, and the disciples to the multitude. And they did all eat and were filled. And they took up of the fragments that remained twelve baskets full. And they that had eaten were about five thousand men, beside women and children.

You know, neighbour, no baker can put up with that; how could he? If it became the custom for anyone who liked to feed five thousand people with five loaves and two small fishes what would become of the bakers, tell me that? It doesn't matter so much about the fishes; they grow of themselves in the water and anyone who likes can catch them. But a baker must buy flour and firewood at a high price, he must employ an assistant and pay him wages; he must keep a shop, he must pay taxes, and this, and that, and by the time he's finished he's glad if he has a few ha'pence left over for himself so that he needn't go begging. And he – he just looks up to heaven and has enough bread for five or I don't know how many thousand people; the flour doesn't cost him anything, he doesn't have to have wood carried long distances, no expenses, no work – well, of course he can give the people bread for nothing! And he never thinks how he's depriving the bakers in the neighbourhood of their hard-earned profits! I tell you it's unfair competition and he ought to be prevented from doing it. Let him pay taxes like us if he wants to run a bakery! People come to us and say, what! you want an extortionate price like that for a wretched little loaf? You ought to give it for nothing, like him; and what bread it is too, so folk say: white and light, and fragrant, so that you can go on and on at it. We've had to bring down our prices as it is; I give you my word, we're selling below cost price simply to avoid having to shut up shop;

if it goes on like it, it'll be the end of the bakery business. I heard that in another place he fed four thousand men, beside women and children, with seven loaves and a few fishes, but that time they only took up four baskets of fragments; so perhaps his business isn't going so well; but he's finished us bakers for good. And I tell you here and now, he only does it from enmity to bakers. The fish-mongers are crying out against him too, but you know they ask outrageous prices for their fish; theirs is not nearly such an honest trade as ours.

Look here, neighbour: I'm only an old fellow and I'm alone in the world; I've neither wife nor children, so what do I need? I told my assistant he could take on my bakery and run it by himself. I don't care about getting on; I tell you I'd really like to give away the modest little bit of property I've got and follow him and cultivate love to my neighbour and all the things he preaches. But when I see the stand he is taking against bakers I say to myself: No you don't! As a baker I see that it is not the redemption of the world but absolute disaster for our business. I'm sorry, but I can't let him get away with it. It won't do.

Of course we lodged a complaint against him with Ananias and with the Governor for interference with trade and for incitement to rebellion; but you know what a time it takes to get the authorities to move. You know me, neighbour; I'm a peaceable man, and I don't seek a quarrel with anyone; but if he comes to Jerusalem I shall stand in the street and shout: Crucify him! Crucify him!

(1937)

Benchanan

Ananias

'YOU ask whether he is guilty, Benchanan. Well, you know, I didn't condemn him to death, I only sent him to Caiaphas. Let Caiaphas tell you what guilt he found in him, I personally have nothing to do with it.

'I'm an old stager, Benchanan, and I will speak to you quite openly. I think that his teaching was sound in parts. The man was right about a lot of things, Benchanan, and he thought honestly; but his tactics were bad. No one could win that way. He should have written it down and published it in a book. People would have read it and said it was a weak or exaggerated book and that there was nothing in it and things like that, the way they always talk about books. But by and by, other people would have started writing the same things, bits taken from it here and there, and others after them, and at least some of it would have taken root. Not all. Not the whole doctrine, but no sensible man would ask that. It's enough if he succeeds in implanting one or two of his ideas. That's how it's done, my dear Benchanan, and it can't be done any other way if we want to reform the world. I tell you, the tactics must be right; what's the good of truth if we can't get people to accept it?

'That was his mistake; he wasn't patient enough. He wanted to redeem the world overnight, even against its will. That doesn't do, Benchanan. He shouldn't have gone

about it so straightforwardly and in such a hurry. Truth
has to sneak in unbeknown; it has to be scattered, a bit
here and a bit there, so that people get accustomed to it
gradually. Not all of a sudden : sell all you have and give
it to the poor, and talk like that. That is a bad method.
For instance, the way he scourged the money-changers out
of the temple – after all, they're good Jews and they have
to make their living somehow. I know the temple isn't the
place for money-changing, but they had always been there
and what could one do about it? He should have lodged a
complaint against them with the synedrium, that would
have been the way. The synedrium could have ordered
them to set their tables a little further away and everything would have been in order. It is always important
how things are done. The man who wants to accomplish
something in the world must never lose his head, he must
control himself, he must always keep his judgement cool
and dispassionate. And those great multitudes of people
that he gathered round him – you know, Benchanan, no
government likes to see that. Or the way he allowed himself to be hailed as king when he rode into Jerusalem; you
have no idea how much bad blood that made. He should
have come on foot, bowing to people here and there –
that's how you have to go about it if you want to have
influence. I even heard that he let himself be entertained
by the Roman tax collector, but I don't believe it, he
wouldn't have done such an ill-advised thing as that; it's
just a piece of malicious gossip. And he shouldn't have
worked those miracles of his; they were bound to shock
people. You see, he couldn't heal everybody, and the
people for whom he had not worked a miracle were
annoyed about it afterwards. Or that business about the
woman taken in adultery – that is said really to have
happened, Benchanan, and it was a terrible mistake. To

tell the people in court that even they were not without
sin – why at that rate one couldn't have any justice in
the world at all. I tell you, he made mistake after mistake.
He should only have taught and not *done* anything, he
shouldn't have taken his teaching so frightfully literally,
he shouldn't have tried to put it into practice at once. He
went about things the wrong way, my dear Benchanan;
between ourselves, he may have been right about a lot of
things, but his tactics were mistaken; so it could only end
one way.

'Don't worry over it, Benchanan; it is all in order. He
was a just man, but if he wanted to save the world, he
shouldn't have gone about it in such an extreme way.
Was he condemned justly, do you say? That is the question! But I tell you, with his tactics he was bound to
fail!'

Caiaphas

'Sit down, my dear Benchanan, I am completely at your
service. So you want to know whether in my opinion the
man was justly crucified? That is a simple matter, my dear
sir. In the first place, it is nothing to do with us, we did
not condemn him to death, did we? We only handed him
over to His Excellency, the Roman Governor. Why should
we assume such a responsibility? If he was justly condemned, well and good; if he has suffered injustice, then
it is the fault of the Romans and some day we may be able
to charge them with it. That's how it is, my dear Benchanan; a matter like this has to be looked at from the
political angle. I, at least, as high priest, have to consider
how it can be turned to account politically. Just reflect,
my friend: the Romans have rid us of a person, who –
how shall I put it? – a person whom for certain reasons

we found undesirable; and yet the responsibility falls upon them.

'What did you say? You want to know what were the reasons? Benchanan, Benchanan, it seems to me that the rising generation has no proper sense of patriotism. Don't you understand how it harms us when someone attacks our recognized authorities such as the Scribes and Pharisees? What will the Romans think of us if this goes on? It tends to undermine the national consciousness! Why, we have to bolster up their prestige for patriotic reasons if we want to prevent our people falling under foreign influences! Anyone who destroys Israel's faith in the Pharisees is playing into the hands of the Romans. And we have managed to get the Romans to execute him themselves: *that* is called policy, Benchanan. And now we find busybodies fussing about whether he was executed justly or no! Remember, young man, your country's interest is above all justice. I know better than anyone else that our Pharisees have their faults; between ourselves, they're a set of gossips and babblers – but all the same we cannot allow anyone to undermine their authority! I know you were his disciple, Benchanan; you liked his doctrine that we must love our neighbours and our enemies and all that kind of talk; but tell me yourself, how did that help us Jews?

'And there's another thing. He shouldn't have said that he came to save the world and that he was the Messiah and the son of God and all that. We all know that he came from Nazareth – what kind of a redeemer is that, I ask you? Why, there are still people who remember him as a carpenter's boy – and does the man think he can reform the world? What next! I am a good Jew, Benchanan, but no one will ever persuade me that one of our people could redeem the world. Man-alive, that would be overestimating ourselves terribly. I wouldn't say anything if it were a Roman or an Egyptian; but an ordinary Jew from Galilee – why, it's ridiculous! Let him tell someone else that he came to save the world, but not us, Benchanan. Not us. Not us.'

(1934)

The Crucifixion

AND Pilate sent for Nahum, a man well versed in history, and learned, and said to him:

'Nahum, it troubles me greatly that your people have resolved to crucify that man. Dammit, man, it's injustice.'

'Without injustice there would be no history,' said Nahum.

'I don't want to have anything to do with it,' said Pilate. 'Tell them to think the matter over.'

'It's too late,' answered Nahum. 'I only follow events in books, so I did not go to see the place of execution; but a moment ago my maidservant came running back from there and said that He has been crucified already and is hanging between two men, one on the right and one on the left.'

Pilate frowned and covered his face with his hands. Presently he said: 'Do not let us speak of it. But tell me, what crime had the man on the right and the man on the left committed?'

'I can't tell you,' answered Nahum; 'some people say they are criminals and others that they are some kind of prophet. As far as I can judge from history, they must have been engaged in politics; but I cannot get it out of my head that the people have crucified them both at the same time.'

'I don't understand you,' said Pilate.

'It's like this,' said Nahum. 'Sometimes the people crucify a man of the right and sometimes a man of the left;

it's always been like that in history. Each period has its martyrs. There are times when they imprison or crucify the man who fights for his nation; and at other times it's the turn of the man who says that one must champion the cause of the poor and the slaves. They alternate, and each has his turn.'

'Aha,' said Pilate. 'So you crucify everyone who champions the cause of something fine.'

'Almost,' said Nahum. 'But there is a snag. Sometimes you'd say that these people are more taken up with their hatred of the others than with the fine things that they proclaim. Men are always crucified for something splendid and great. The man who is on the cross is sacrificing his life for something great; but the man who drags him to the cross and nails him there, Pilate, is evil and mad and therefore hideous to look upon. Pilate, the people is a great and beautiful thing.'

'Our Roman people is,' said Pilate.

'Ours, too,' said Nahum. 'But justice for the poor is also a great and beautiful thing. Only these people manage to choke themselves to death with their hatred and rage against these great and beautiful things; and the remaining ones go first with one side and then with the other and always help to crucify the man whose turn it is; or else they just look on and say: Serves him right, he should have joined our side.'

'Then why do they crucify the one in the centre?' asked Pilate.

'Well, you see,' Nahum explained, 'if the one on the left wins he crucifies the one on the right, but first he crucifies the one in the centre. If the one on the right wins he crucifies the one on the left, but first the one in the centre. Of course it may also happen that there are disorders and fighting; then the one on the right and the one on the left make common cause and crucify the one in the centre because he did not make up his mind which of the two to oppose. If you went up on to the roof of your house you would see the field of Haceldama: hatred on the left, hatred on the right, and between them Him who sought to rule by love and reason, so they tell of Him. And besides that you would see a multitude of people just looking on while they eat their dinner which they have brought with them. The sky is darkening; now they are all hurrying home helter-skelter so as not to get their clothes wet.'

And when it was the sixth hour there was darkness over all the land until the ninth hour. And about the ninth hour He who was in the centre cried with a loud voice, saying: 'Eloi, Eloi lama sabachthani?' And behold, the veil of the temple was rent in twain from the top to the bottom; and the earth did quake and the rocks were rent.

(1927)

Pilate's Evening

THAT evening Pilate supped with his adjutant, young lieutenant Suza of a family from Cyrenaica. Suza did not notice that the Governor was rather out of humour, but chattered away in high spirits, excited at having been in an earthquake for the first time in his life.

'It was a perfect scream,' he exclaimed between mouthfuls. 'When it got dark like that after dinner, I ran out to see what was up. On the stairs my legs suddenly twitched and seemed to give way under me – it was too funny for words. Honestly, Excellency, it never occurred to me that a little thing like that was an earthquake. And before I was round the corner some civilians came rushing up to me with their eyes popping out of their heads, yelling: "The graves are opening and the rocks are rent!" By Jupiter! I said to myself, was that an earthquake? Well, that was a stroke of luck! It's a fairly rare phenomenon, isn't it, sir?'

Pilate nodded. 'I saw an earthquake once before,' he said. 'That was in Cilicia. Let's see, it will be seventeen years ago or thereabouts. It was a bigger one.'

'Nothing much happened, when all's said and done,' Suza remarked carelessly. 'At the gate towards Haceldama a piece of rock fell down – oh yes, and a few graves opened in the graveyard. I'm surprised they bury the dead so near the surface, hardly a cubit deep. Of course they stink in summer.'

'Custom,' grunted Pilate. 'In Persia, for instance, they

don't bury the dead at all. They simply lay them in the sun.'

'It ought to be forbidden, sir,' said Suza, 'for reasons of health and so on.'

'If you once begin that,' objected Pilate, 'then you're continually having to order and forbid things; that's bad policy, Suza. Don't interfere in their affairs – then at least there's peace and quiet. If they want to live like beasts, let them. Ah, Suza, I have seen so many countries.'

'What I want to know,' Suza returned to his main interest, 'is what causes one of these earthquakes? Perhaps there are sort of holes under the earth which suddenly fall in. But why did the sky go so dark while it was going on? It doesn't make sense to me. The morning looked as clear as usual . . .'

'Begging your pardon, sir,' said old Papadokitis, a Greek from the Dodecanese who was waiting on them, 'it had been expected since yesterday, sir. Yesterday there was such a red sunset, sir, and I said to Myriam the cook, to-morrow there'll be a storm or a hurricane. I've a pain in the small of my back, I said to Myriam. Something was bound to happen. Begging your pardon, sir.'

'Something was bound to happen,' repeated Pilate thoughtfully. 'Do you know, Suza, I was expecting something today, too. Ever since this morning when I handed over the man from Nazareth to those people. I had to hand him over because Roman policy refrains on principle from interfering in local affairs – remember that, Suza. The less the people have to do with the supreme authority, the more ready they are to put up with it – by Jupiter, what was I talking about?'

'About the man from Nazareth,' Suza reminded him.

'About the man from Nazareth. You know, Suza, I was rather interested in him. He was born in Bethlehem. I consider that the natives here were guilty of judicial murder in his case, but that's their affair. If I hadn't handed him over they'd certainly have torn him to pieces and that would only have brought the Roman administration into bad odour. No, wait a minute, that's not what I meant to say. Ananias told me that he is considered a dangerous man; it is said that when he was born the shepherds of Bethlehem came and knelt to him as to a king. And not long ago the people here welcomed him as one that comes in triumph. I can't get the idea out of my head, Suza. I should have thought –'

'What did you think?' Suza prompted him after a while.

'I thought that perhaps his own people would come from Bethlehem. That they wouldn't leave him in the clutches of these intriguers here. I thought they'd come to me and say: "Sir, he belongs to us and means something to us, so we've come to tell you that we stand behind him and we're not going to see him wronged." – Suza, I was almost looking forward to those mountain folk; I'm thoroughly sick of the pettifogging hair-splitters here – And I would have said to them: "Thank God you have come, men of Bethlehem. I was expecting you. On his account and also because of yourselves and your country. One can't govern talking dummies; one can only govern men, not talk. Men like you can be made into soldiers who stand fast; men like you can be made into nations and states. They tell me that this countryman of yours brings the dead to life. Now why the dead? But you are here, and I see that he can bring even the living to life; that he has imbued you with loyalty and honour and – we Romans call it *virtus*. I don't know what it's called in your language, men of Bethlehem, but it is in you. I think this man will do some fine things yet. It would be a pity to waste him."'

Pilate fell silent and absentmindedly swept the crumbs from the table. 'Well, they didn't come,' he sighed. 'Ah, Suza, what a vain thing it is to govern.'

Pilate's Creed

Jesus answered, To this end was I born, and for this cause came I into the world, that I should bear witness unto the truth. Every one that is of the truth heareth my voice.

Pilate saith unto him, What is truth? and when he had said this, he went out again unto the Jews, and saith unto them, I find in him no fault at all.

(John xviii. 37–8)

TOWARDS evening a certain man called Joseph of Arimathea, who was much respected in the city and was also a disciple of Christ, came to Pilate and besought him to give him the body of Jesus. Pilate consented and said: 'He was executed wrongfully.'

'You yourself handed Him over to death,' protested Joseph.

'Yes, I did,' answered Pilate, 'and of course people think I did it for fear of those windbags who were shouting for their Barabbas. If I'd sent five soldiers against them it would have silenced them. But that's not the point, Joseph of Arimathea.

'That's not the point,' he went on after a pause. 'But when I was talking with him I saw that after a time his disciples will crucify others: in the name of his name, in the name of his truth they will crucify and torture everyone else, they will kill other truths and raise other Barabbases on their shoulders. The man spoke of truth. What is truth?

'You are a strange people and you talk a great deal. You

have all sorts of pharisees, prophets, redeemers and other sectarians. Each one who makes his own truth rules out all the other truths. As though a carpenter who makes a new chair were to forbid people to sit on other chairs which anyone had made before him. As though the making of a new chair abolished all the old chairs. It is indeed possible that the new chair is better, more beautiful and more comfortable than the others; but why in heaven's name should a tired man not be able to sit down on any wretched worm-eaten or stone seat? He is tired and broken, he needs a rest; and here you drag him by force from the resting-place into which he has dropped to make him change over to yours. I do not understand you, Joseph.'

'Truth,' objected Joseph of Arimathea, 'is not like a chair and a resting-place; it is rather like a command which says: Go here and there, do this and that; defeat the enemy, conquer that city, punish treachery and so forth. The man who does not obey such a command is a traitor and an enemy. That's how it is with truth.'

'Ah, Joseph,' said Pilate, 'you know I am a soldier and have lived the greater part of my life among soldiers. I have always obeyed orders, but not because they were the truth. The truth was that I was tired or thirsty; that I was homesick for my mother or eager for fame; that this soldier was thinking of his wife and that one of his field or oxen. The truth was that if there had been no command none of these soldiers would have gone to kill other people as tired and unhappy as themselves. Then what is truth? I believe that at least we hold a little of the truth if we think of the soldiers and not of the command.'

'Truth is not the order of a commander,' said Joseph of Arimathea, 'but the command of reason. You know that this column is white; if I were to tell you it was black, that would be contrary to your reason and you would not agree that I was right.'

'Why not?' asked Pilate. 'I should say to myself that perhaps you were frightfully unhappy and depressed if a white column looked black to you; I should try to distract you; in fact I should be more interested in you than before. And even if it were only a mistake I should say to myself that your mistake contains as much of your soul as your truth.'

'It is not *my* truth,' said Joseph of Arimathea. 'There is only one truth for all.'

'And which is that?'

'The truth in which I believe.'

'There, you see,' said Pilate slowly. 'It is only *your* truth after all. You are like little children who believe that the whole world ends with their horizon and that there is nothing more beyond. The world is a large place, Joseph, and there is room in it for many things. I think there is actually room in it for many truths. Look, I am a stranger in these parts and my home is far beyond the horizon; yet I should not say that this country is wrong. Equally strange to me is the doctrine of this Jesus of yours; but am I therefore to say that it is wrong? I think, Joseph, that all countries are right; but the world has to be tremendously vast for them all to fit in beside each other and behind each other. If Arabia had to stand on the same spot as Pontus, of course it would not be right. And it is the same with truths. The world would have to be made enormously vast, spacious and free for all the real truths to fit into it. And I think it is, Joseph. When you climb a very high mountain you see that things merge into each other and flatten out into a single plain. From a certain height truths merge into each other. Of course man does not live and cannot live on the top of a high mountain; it is enough for him if he sees his house or his fields close to, both of them full of truths and facts; that is his true place and sphere of action. But now and then he can look at the mountains or the sky and say to himself that from there his truth and his things still exist and nothing of them is stolen, but they merge with something far freer which is no longer his property. To keep this vast view while tilling his little field – that, Joseph, is something almost like prayer. And I think that the heavenly Father of such a man really exists somewhere but that he gets on quite well with Apollo and the other gods. They are partly merged in each other and partly side by side. Look, there is an enormous lot of room in heaven. I am glad the heavenly Father is there too.'

'You are neither hot nor cold,' said Joseph of Arimathea, rising. 'You are just luke-warm.'

'No,' answered Pilate. 'I believe, I believe most passionately that truth exists and that man recognizes it. It would be madness to think that truth is only there for man not to know it. He knows it, yes; but who? I or you, or maybe everyone? I believe that each one of us has a share of it; the man who says yes and the man who says no. If these two united and understood each other that would give the whole of truth. Of course, yes and no cannot unite, but people always can; there is more truth in people than in words. I have more understanding of people than of their truths; but there is faith even in that, Joseph of Arimathea : faith and the need to hold oneself in enthusiasm and rapture. I believe. I believe absolutely and unhesitatingly. But what is truth?'

(1920)

The Emperor Diocletian

THIS story would certainly be more impressive if its heroine were Diocletian's daughter or some other youthful and girlish creature; but alas, for reasons of historical accuracy it is Diocletian's sister, an elderly and imposing matron, somewhat hysterical and highly strung in the emperor's opinion, of whom the old tyrant was rather afraid. So when she was announced he interrupted an audience with the governor of Cyrenaica (to whom he expressed his displeasure in strong terms) and advanced as far as the door to meet her.

'Well, what is it, Antonia?' he boomed jovially. 'What do you want? Have you another penniless protégé? Or am I to do something to prevent cruelty to animals in the circus? Or do you want to introduce moral education in the Legion? Out with it quickly, and do sit down.'

But Antonia continued to stand. 'Diocletian,' she began almost ceremoniously, 'there is something I *must* say to you.'

'Aha,' said the emperor resignedly and scratched the back of his neck. 'But by Jupiter, I've got such a lot to do today. Couldn't it wait till another time?'

'Diocletian,' his sister continued obstinately, 'I have come to tell you that you *must* stop this persecution of the Christians.'

'Look here,' grunted the old emperor, 'why this all of a sudden – after about three hundred years –' He looked attentively at the agitated matron; she looked rather pathetic with her austere eyes and convulsively clasped hands which were twisted by gout. 'Oh, all right,' he said quickly, 'we can have a talk about it; but first do sit down, there's a good girl.'

Antonia obeyed mechanically and sat down on the edge of a chair; this made her lose a little of her fighting posture, she seemed smaller and softer; the corners of her mouth trembled as if she were going to cry. 'These people are so holy, Diocletian,' she burst out, 'and they have such a beautiful faith. I know if you knew them – Diocletian, you *must* get to know them! You'll see that – that then you'll have quite a different opinion of them –'

'But I haven't a bad opinion of them at all,' protested Diocletian mildly. 'I know that what's said about them is idle gossip and slander. It's invented by our augurers – you know, professional jealousy and all that. I have had inquiries made and I hear that these Christians are otherwise quite decent people. Very well-behaved and self-sacrificing.'

'Then why do you persecute them so?' asked Antonia in astonishment.

Diocletian raised his eyebrows a little. 'Why? What a question! It's always been done, hasn't it? And yet there's no sign of there being fewer of them. This talk about persecution is frightfully exaggerated. Of course, now and then we have to punish a few of them as an example –'

'Why?' repeated Antonia.

'For political reasons,' said the old emperor. 'Look here, my dear, I could give you a whole lot of reasons. For instance, the people like it. Firstly, because it diverts their attention from other things. Secondly, it gives them a comfortable feeling that they are ruled by a strong hand. And, thirdly, it's more or less a national custom here. I tell you, no sensible and responsible statesman interferes unnecessarily in matters of custom. That only arouses a feeling of insecurity and – hm – well, upheaval. My dear girl, I've introduced more innovations during my rule than anyone ever did before. But they were necessary. When it isn't necessary, I don't do it.'

'But justice, Diocletian,' said Antonia softly, 'justice is necessary. I demand justice of you.'

Diocletian shrugged his shoulders. 'The persecution of the Christians is just because it is in accordance with the laws in force. I know what's on the tip of your tongue: that I could alter the laws. I could, but I'm not going to. My dear Toni, remember, *minima non curat praetor*; I can't trouble about such trifles. Be good enough to bear in mind that I've the whole administration of the empire on my shoulders; and I have altered it from its very foundations, my girl. I've reframed the constitution, I've reformed the senate, centralized the administration, reorganized the whole bureaucracy, divided the provinces on a new principle, revised their administrative system – all these are things which *had* to be done in the interest of the state. You're a woman and don't understand; but the gravest tasks of a statesman are administrative. Just you tell me, what do these Christians matter compared with – with – well, with the establishment of imperial financial control? It's nonsense!'

'But Diocletian,' breathed Antonia, 'you could so easily arrange –'

'I could. And then again I couldn't,' said the emperor with decision. 'I have placed the whole empire on an entirely new administrative footing – and the people have hardly noticed it. Because I have left them their customs. When I give them a few Christians they have the impression that everything is going on in the good old way and they leave me in peace. My dearest girl, a statesman has to know how far he can venture with his reforms. That's how it is.'

'Then it's only,' said Antonia bitterly, 'only so that you may be left in peace by these people here who haven't enough to do and are always clamouring about something –'

Diocletian made a grimace. 'If you like. But I tell you I've read books by these Christians of yours that have made me think a bit.'

'And what have you found in them that was bad?' cried Antonia fiercely.

'Bad?' said the emperor thoughtfully. 'On the contrary, there's quite a lot in it. Love and things like that – even this scorn of worldly vanities – Really they're quite beautiful ideals and if I weren't emperor – You know, Toni, some things in their doctrine I liked tremendously; if only I had more time – and could think about my soul –' The old emperor thumped the table excitedly with his fist. 'But it's absurd. Absolutely impossible politically. It can't be carried out. Can you really make a Kingdom of God? How is it to be administered? By love? By the word of God? I know something about people, don't I? Politically the doctrine is so immature and impracticable that – that – that it's absolutely criminal.'

'But they don't have anything to do with politics,' countered Antonia hotly. 'And there's not a word about it in their holy books.'

'For the practical statesman,' said Diocletian, 'everything is politics. Everything has a political significance. Every idea must be weighed politically to see how it could be carried out, what should be done about it, where it would lead. Day after day, night after night I have cudgelled my brains to discover how the Christian doctrine could be carried out politically; and I see that it is impossible. I tell you, a Christian State could not hold together for a month. Tell me, can you organize an army on Christian lines? Can you raise taxes on Christian lines? Could there be slaves in a Christian society? I know what I'm talking about, Toni; one couldn't govern on Christian principles for a year, not for a month. That's why Christianity will never take root. It may be the faith of artisans and slaves, but it can never, never be a State religion. That's out of the question. You know, those ideas of theirs about property, about one's neighbour, about the reprehensibility of all violence and all the rest of it, they're beautiful but impossible in practice. They won't do in real life, Toni. What do *you* think about them?'

'They may be impossible,' murmured Antonia, 'but that doesn't make them criminal.'

'Criminal,' said the emperor, 'means something which harms the State. And Christianity would overthrow the supreme power of the State. That won't do. The supreme power, my dear, must be in this world, not the next. When I say that a Christian State is not possible in principle it follows as a logical conclusion that the State cannot tolerate Christianity. The responsible statesman must take moderate measure against unhealthy and unrealizable dreams. In any case, they're only the illusions of madmen and slaves –'

Antonia rose to her feet and took a deep breath. 'Diocletian, I must tell you that I have become a Christian.'

'Go on!' said the emperor in mild astonishment. 'Well, why not? Didn't I say there was something in it? and so long as it remains your personal affair – You mustn't think, Toni, that I have no understanding of these things. I should like to be a human soul again for once. Toni, I should like to put off my imperial state and politics and all that and hang it on a hook on the wall – that is when once I've finished the reform of the imperial administration and a few jobs like that; and then, then I'd go away somewhere in the country and study Plato – Christ – Marcus Aurelius – and that Paul of theirs or whatever he calls himself – But excuse me now; I've got a political conference.'

(1932)

Attila

EARLY in the morning a messenger brought news from the forest country that a great sea of fire had been burning all night to the south-east. All that day again a raw drizzle fell, the damp firewood would not catch alight; three of the multitude died of a bloody flux. Because there was nothing to eat two of the men set off on a journey to the shepherds in the land beyond the forest; late in the afternoon they returned, soaked to the skin and utterly exhausted. They just managed to gasp out that things were bad; the sheep were dying in convulsions and the cows were swollen with wind; the shepherds had fallen upon them with clubs and knives when one of them wanted to take away his own heifer which he had placed in their care before he fled to the forest.

'Let us pray,' said the priest, who was suffering from dysentery. 'The Lord will have mercy.'

'*Kriste eleison*,' the dejected multitude began to chant through their noses. At this moment a screaming brawl broke out among the women over a ragged piece of woollen cloth.

'What's the matter now, you accursed hags?' roared the head man, and strode among the women, lashing out with his whip. This eased the tension of despair, the men began to feel like men again.

'Those plainsmen won't get as far as this,' declared a man with a flowing beard. 'Not into these narrow ravines among all this underbrush. People say their horses are as small and scraggy as goats.'

'What I say is we ought to have stayed in the city,' objected an excited little man. 'Think of all the money we spent on those fortifications ... For that money the walls could be as strong as a rock, now couldn't they?'

'Well, well,' chuckled a consumptive clerk. 'For all that money the walls could be made of cake. You go and have a bite – plenty of people have been gorging on it, man; maybe there's a bit left for you.'

The head man gave a warning cough; this conversation was obviously not to his taste.

'What I say is,' the excited little townsman persisted obstinately, 'cavalry against walls like that ... Don't let them into the city and there you are. And we should have had a dry roof over our heads.'

'Well, go back to the city and crawl into bed,' the bearded man advised him.

'What should I do there all by myself?' objected the excited man. 'I'm only saying we should have stayed in the city and defended ourselves ... I've the right to say we've made a mistake, haven't I? Those fortifications have cost us a mint of money and now they say they're no use! Well, I ask you!'

'However things are,' said the priest, 'we must trust in God's help. My people, this Attila is only a pagan –'

'The scourge of God,' exclaimed a monk, shaking with ague. 'The chastisement of God.'

The men relapsed into grumpy silence; this feverish monk would only go on preaching and he didn't even belong to their parish. What have we got our parish priest for? they thought. He belongs to us, he puts up with us and isn't always denouncing our sins. As though we sinned so very much, thought the men gloomily.

The rain stopped but heavy drops still plopped down from the tree-tops. 'Lord, Lord, Lord,' groaned the priest, wrung by his sickness.

Towards evening the sentries dragged in a wretched youth who said he was a refugee from the enemy-occupied country to the east.

The mayor puffed out his chest and began to interrogate the refugee; he was obviously of the opinion that an official matter of this sort must be carried out with great severity. Yes, said the youth, the Huns are only eleven miles from here and are advancing slowly. They occupied his town, he saw them – no, he did not see Attila but he saw another general, a fat one. Did they set fire to the town? No, they didn't; the fat general issued a proclamation that nothing would happen to the civilian population but that the town must provide fodder, food and various other things. And the inhabitants must refrain from hostile remarks about the Huns, otherwise he would proceed to the severest reprisals.

'But these pagans slaughter even the women and children,' insisted the bearded man firmly.

The boy had been told they didn't. Not in his town. He himself had been hidden under the straw, but when his mother told him people were saying that the Huns were going to carry off the young men to tend their flocks and herds, he escaped by night. That was all he knew.

The men were dissatisfied. 'But it's known that they cut off the hands of infants,' declared one of them, 'and what they do to the women doesn't bear speaking of.'

'I don't know about anything like that,' said the youth, as if excusing himself. At least, it wasn't as bad as that in his town. And how many Huns were there? he was asked. People said about two hundred, there wouldn't be more.

'You're lying!' cried the man with the flowing beard. 'Why, everybody knows that there are more than five hundred thousand of them. And wherever they come they slaughter and pillage till nothing remains.'

'They lock the people into the stables and set fire to them,' said another.

'And they toss the infants from the points of their spears,' put in a third excitedly.

'And roast them over the flames,' added a fourth with a streaming cold. 'The accursed pagans!'

'Lord, Lord!' groaned the priest. 'Lord have mercy upon us!'

'You seem to me to be a queer fellow,' the bearded man said suspiciously to the boy. 'How can you say you have seen the Huns when you were hidden in the straw?'

'Mother saw them,' stammered the boy, 'and she came up to the loft to bring me something to eat –'

'You're lying!' thundered the man with the long beard. 'We know that wherever the Huns come they devour everything like locusts. Not a leaf is left on the trees where they have passed, do you understand?'

'God in heaven, God in heaven!' the excited little townsman began to whimper. 'And why? why is it? Who is to blame? Who sent them here? We have paid out so much for the army . . . God in heaven!'

'Who sent them here?' asked the clerk derisively. 'Don't you know that? You ask His Majesty the Byzantine Emperor who summoned those yellow monkeys here! Why, man, everyone knows today who's paying for the wanderings of peoples! They call it high politics, that's what they call it.'

The mayor cleared his throat in an important manner. 'Nonsense. It's not like that at all. These Huns are probably dying of hunger at home . . . they're a lazy rabble

... don't know how to work ... have no civilization ... and they want to gorge themselves full. That's why they come to us ... to seize our things ... the fruits of our labour. Just to plunder, divide the spoils ... and then move on, the miserable wretches!'

'They are uncivilized pagans,' said the priest. 'A wild and unenlightened people. God has only sent them to try us; let us pray and give thanks and things will all come right again.'

'The scourge of God,' cried the feverish monk emotionally, beginning to preach a sermon. 'God will punish you for your sins, God will lead the Huns and will wipe you from the face of the earth like the people of Sodom. For your lustfulness and blaspheming, for the hardness and godlessness of your hearts, for your avarice and gluttony, for your sinful wealth and your worship of Mammon, God has cast you off and delivered you into the hands of your enemies!'

The mayor cleared his throat threateningly. 'Mind what you're saying, Domine; you're not in church now, you know. They've come to have a good feed. They're starving, tattered ruffians ...'

'It's politics,' insisted the clerk obstinately. 'Byzantium has got a finger in it.'

A man with blackened face and arms, a tinker by trade, burst out passionately: 'Byzantium? not a bit of it! It's those kettle-menders have done it and no one else! Three years ago a strolling kettle-mender came here and he had a little shaggy horse exactly like those the Huns have got.'

'And what of it?' asked the mayor.

'Why, it stands to reason,' shouted the man with the blackened face. 'The kettle-menders came on in front to spy out everything ... they were spies ... It's the kettle-menders who have hatched this plot! Does anyone know

where they came from? Or what they wanted here?
What did they come for ... what use were they when
there was a regular tinker living in the town? Just spoiling
our trade ... and spying ... They never went to church
a single time ... they worked spells ... they laid the evil
eye on the beasts ... they drew the harlots after them ...
It's all the doing of the kettle-menders!'

'There's something in that,' observed the man with the
flowing beard. 'Kettle-menders are strange folk; it's said
they even eat raw meat.'

'They're a gang of thieves,' declared the mayor. 'They
steal chickens and anything else they can lay their hands
on.'

The tinker choked with righteous wrath. 'There, you
see! They say it's Attila, but the kettle-menders are behind it! They're at the bottom of it all, the accursed
kettle-menders! They've cast spells on our beasts ...
they've sent the dysentery to us ... It's all the kettle-
menders! You ought to hang each one of them wherever
he shows his face! Why, don't you know ... don't you
know about the cauldrons of Hell? And haven't you
heard that the Huns beat on pots and pans when they're
advancing. A child could see the connection! It's the
kettle-menders who have brought the war upon us ...
they are to blame for it all ... And you,' he shouted,
foaming at the mouth and pointing at the stranger youth,
'you're a kettle-mender too, you're an ally and a spy of the
kettle-menders! That's why you've come ... and you're
trying to trick us, you want to betray us to the kettle-
menders...'

'Hang him!' shrieked the excited little man.

'Wait, neighbours,' the mayor thundered above the
tumult. 'This must be inquired into ... Silence!'

'Hang him without more ado!' yelled someone.

Even the women began hurrying to the spot.

*

That night the fiery glow was seen to the north-west. It drizzled on and off. Five of the multitude died of dysentery and coughs.

The stranger youth was hanged after he had been tortured for some time.

(1932)

The Idol Breakers

A CERTAIN Prokopios, well known as an expert connoisseur and enthusiastic collector of Byzantine art, had come to see Nikeforos, Superior of the Monastery of St Simeon. Prokopios was visibly moved as he waited, walking up and down the cloisters. Beautiful pillars they have here, he thought, obviously fifth century. Nikeforos is the only man who can help us. He has influence at court and used to be a painter himself. And the old man wasn't a bad painter either. I remember he used to make embroidery designs for the Empress and paint ikons for her. That's why they made him abbot when his hands got so twisted with gout that he couldn't hold a paint-brush. And they say his word still carries weight at court. Lord Jesus, that's a beautiful capital! Yes, Nikeforos will help us. It's a good thing we thought of him!

'Welcome, Prokopios,' said a soft voice behind him.

Prokopios turned abruptly. Behind him stood a wrinkled gracious little old man with his hands wrapped in his sleeves. 'A beautiful capital, isn't it?' he said. 'Ancient work from Naxos, sir.'

Prokopios kissed the abbot's sleeve. 'I have come to you, Father,' he began with emotion, but the abbot interrupted him.

'Come and sit in the sunshine, my dear son. It is good for my gout. What a day, dear God, what light! Now, what brings you to me?' he asked when they were seated on a stone seat in the middle of the monastery garden, full of the murmur of bees and the scent of sage, thyme and mint.

'Father,' burst out Prokopios, 'I have come to you as the only man who can avert a grievous and irreparable disaster to culture. I know that in you I shall find understanding. You are an artist, Father. What a painter you used to be until you were called upon to bear upon your shoulders the burden of your spiritual office ! God forgive me, but I sometimes regret that you did not remain bent over the wooden panels on which you used to conjure up some of the most beautiful of Byzantine ikons.'

Instead of replying, Father Nikeforos turned back the sleeves of his robe and laid his poor, knotted hands, twisted by the gout like a parrot's claws, in the sun. 'Oh no,' he said simply. 'What are you saying, my dear son !'

'It is the truth, Nikeforos,' said Prokopios. (Holy Virgin, what dreadful hands !) 'Your ikons are priceless today. Only the other day a Jew asked two thousand drachmas for one of your pictures, and when he didn't get his price he said he would wait and in ten years it would fetch three times as much.'

Father Nikeforos coughed modestly and flushed with immense pleasure. 'You don't say so !' he murmured. 'Now, who could be talking about my modest paintings? There is no need, I'm sure; you have such popular masters, men like Argyropulos, Malvasias, Papadanios, Megalo- kastros and so on, for instance, that man who does those mosaics – what is his name?'

'Do you mean Papanastasias?' asked Prokopios.

'Yes, yes,' grunted Nikeforos. 'They say he has a great reputation. Now, I don't know; but I should have been more inclined to call mosaics stone-mason's work than real painting. They say that this man of yours – now, what is his name –?'

'Papanastasias?'

'Yes, Papanastasias. They say he is a Cretan. In my day we had a different view of the Cretan school. Not a good style, they said. The lines are too hard, and those colours! You say that this Cretan is tremendously admired? Hm, extraordinary.'

'I never said anything of the sort,' protested Prokopios. 'But have you seen his latest mosaics?'

Father Nikeforos shook his head with decision. 'No, no, my dear son. What should I look at them for? Lines like wires, and that glaring gold! Have you noticed that in his latest mosaic the Archangel Gabriel is standing tilted right over as if he were falling? Why, this Cretan of yours can't even draw a figure so that it stands properly!'

'Well,' suggested Prokopios dubiously, 'perhaps he did it intentionally, for reasons of composition –'

'I never heard such nonsense!' burst out the abbot, and puffed out his angry face. 'Reasons of composition! So one can draw badly for reasons of composition, can one? And the Emperor himself goes and looks at it and says, "interesting, very interesting"!' Father Nikeforos mastered his anger. 'Draughtsmanship, sir, draughtsmanship before everything; the whole of art is in that.'

'Those are the words of a master,' Prokopios hastened to propitiate him. 'I have your Ascension in my collection, but I tell you, Father, I would not let it go, even in exchange for a Nikaon.'

'Nikaon was a good painter,' said Nikeforos with decision. 'The classical school, sir. What beautiful proportions! But my Ascension is a poor picture, Prokopios. Those motionless figures and the Christ with wings like a stork – Why, man, Christ must float in the air without wings! That is art!' Father Nikeforos wiped his nose on his sleeve with emotion. 'It can't be helped. I didn't know how to draw *then*. The picture had no depth, no movement.'

Prokopios stared at the abbot's twisted hands in astonishment. 'Father, do you still paint?'

Father Nikeforos shook his head. 'No. Oh, no. Only now and then I just try something for my own pleasure.'

'Figures?' burst out Prokopios.

'Figures. My son, nothing is more beautiful than figures. Standing figures which look as if they were about to step forward. And a background behind them into which you would say they could retreat. It is difficult, my friend. What does that man of yours – what is his name? – that mason from Crete – know about it with his distorted puppets?'

'I should like to see your new pictures, Nikeforos,' said Prokopios.

Father Nikeforos waved his hand. 'Why? You have your Papanastasias, haven't you? A magnificent artist, you say. He and his reasons of composition ! Well, if his mosaic figures are art then I don't know what painting is. You are a connoisseur, of course, Prokopios; you may be right that Papanastasias is a genius.'

'I didn't say that,' protested Prokopios. 'Nikeforos, I did not come to argue with you about art but to save it before it is too late.'

'From Papanastasias?' asked Nikeforos eagerly.

'No, from the Emperor. You know about it, of course. His Majesty the Emperor Constantine Copronymos, under pressure from certain ecclesiastical circles, is going to forbid the painting of ikons. It is said to be idolatry or something. Such nonsense, Nikeforos !'

The abbot veiled his eyes with his faded lashes. 'I heard about it, Prokopios,' he murmured. 'But it isn't certain. No, it is not decided yet.'

'That is why I have come to you, Father,' said Prokopios eagerly. 'Everyone knows that for the Emperor it is a purely political question. He doesn't care a damn about idolatry but he wants peace and quiet. And when a rabble led by dirty fanatics rushes after him in the streets shouting "away with the idols", our illustrious ruler naturally thinks that the most comfortable way is to give in to the hairy mob. Did you know that they had painted out the frescoes in the Chapel of Supreme Love?'

'I heard about it,' sighed the abbot with closed eyes. 'What a sin, Mother of God! Such exquisite frescoes from the hand of Stefanides himself! Do you remember the figure of St Sofia to the left of the Christ with his hand raised in benediction? Prokopios, that was the most beautiful standing figure I have ever seen. Yes, Stefanides was a master, say what you will!'

Prokopios leaned urgently towards the abbot. 'Nikeforos, it is written in the Law of Moses: Thou shalt not make unto thyself graven images in the likeness of anything that is in the heavens above nor in the earth beneath nor in the waters under the earth. Nikeforos, are they right who declare that it is forbidden of God to paint pictures and carve statues?'

Father Nikeforos shook his head without opening his eyes. 'Prokopios,' he sighed after a time, 'art is as holy as religion, for ... it glorifies the works of God ... and teaches us to love them.' He made the sign of the cross in the air with his crippled hand. 'Was not the Creator Himself an artist? Did He not model the form of man from the clay of the earth? Did He not give to every object outline and colour? And what an artist, Prokopios! Never, never can we learn enough from Him – Besides, that law was only laid down for barbarous times when people could not draw properly.'

Prokopios gave a deep sigh of relief. 'I knew that you would speak like this, Father,' he said respectfully. 'As a priest – and as an artist. Nikeforos, you will not allow works of art to be destroyed!'

The abbot opened his eyes. 'I? What can I do, Prokopios? Times are bad; the cultivated world is adopting barbaric customs, people are coming from Crete and from God knows where. It is terrible, my friend; but how can we avert it?'

'Nikeforos, if you spoke to the Emperor –'

'No, no,' said Father Nikeforos. 'I cannot speak to the Emperor. You know he has no feeling for art, Prokopios. I have heard that recently he praised the mosaics by that man of yours – now, what was his name?'

'Papanastasias, Father.'

'Yes. The man who does those figures all out of drawing. The Emperor has no conception what art is. And in my opinion Malvasias is an equally bad painter. The school of Ravenna, you know. And in spite of that they gave him the mosaics in the court chapel to do! No, there's nothing to be done at court, Prokopios. I can't go there and beg them to allow a man like Argyropulos or that Cretan fellow – Papanastasias is it? – to go on spoiling the walls!'

'It's not that, Father,' said Prokopios patiently. 'But consider – if the idol-breakers succeed, all art will be destroyed. Even your ikons will be burned, Nikeforos!'

The abbot waved his hand. 'They weren't good, Prokopios,' he murmured. 'I couldn't draw then. Drawing figures, sir, is not learned in five minutes.'

With a trembling finger Prokopios pointed to an antique statue of a young Bacchus half covered by a briar rose in blossom. 'That statue will be smashed as well,' he said.

'What a sin, what a sin,' whispered Nikeforos, half closing his eyes in pain. 'We called that statue St John the Baptist, but it is a real, perfect Bacchus. I sit here and gaze at it for hours on end. It is like praying, Prokopios.'

'There, you see, Nikeforos. And is that divine perfection to be destroyed for ever? Is some verminous, howling fanatic to smash it to fragments with a hammer?'

The abbot sat silent with his hands folded.

'You can save art itself, Nikeforos,' said Prokopios in urgent persuasion. 'Your holy life and your wisdom have won you immense respect in the Church; the court esteems you highly; you will be a member of the Great Synod which will decide whether all statues and pictures are simply tools of idolatry. Father, the fate of all art is in your hands!'

'You overestimate my influence, Prokopios,' sighed the abbot. 'These fanatics are strong, and they have the mob behind them –' Nikeforos was silent. 'Did you say they would destroy all the pictures and statues?'

'Yes.'

'And would they destroy the mosaics too?'

'Yes. They would tear them from the ceilings and throw the stones on the rubbish heap.'

'Really?' asked Nikeforos with interest. 'Then they would tear down that badly drawn Archangel Gabriel by that man – er –'

'I suppose so.'

'That's a good thing,' chuckled the abbot. 'It's a terribly bad picture. I have never seen such an impossible figure; and to say it's for reasons of composition! I tell you, Prokopios, bad drawing is a sin and a blasphemy; it is an offence against God. And are the people to kneel before it? No, no! The truth is that to kneel to bad pictures is real idolatry. I am not surprised that the people have risen against it in anger. They are quite right. The Cretan school is fallacious; and a man like Papanastasias is a worse heretic than any Arian. So you say they would tear down those worthless scrawls?' asked the abbot happily. 'You bring me good news, my dear son. I am glad that you came.' Nikeforos rose to his feet with an effort as a sign that the audience was at an end. 'Beautiful weather we are having, aren't we?'

Prokopios stood up, visibly crushed. 'But Nikeforos,' he burst out, almost in tears, 'other pictures will be destroyed as well. Listen. All works of art will be burned or smashed to pieces.'

'There, there,' said the abbot soothingly. 'It's a pity, a great pity. But if the world is to be rid of bad drawings we must not look too closely at an accident here and there. So long as the people don't have to kneel to figures all out of drawing like the things that that man – now what –?'

'Papanastasias.'

'Yes, that's the man. The Cretan school is thoroughly bad, Prokopios. I am glad you drew my attention to the Synod. I shall be there, Prokopios, I shall be there even if they have to carry me. I should reproach myself to my dying day if I were not present. If only they tear down that Archangel Gabriel,' said Nikeforos, smiling all over his wrinkled face. 'God be with you, my son,' he ended, raising his crippled hand in blessing.

'God be with you, Nikeforos,' sighed Prokopios despairingly.

Abbot Nikeforos walked away shaking his head thoughtfully. 'The Cretan school is bad,' he muttered. 'It's high time it was put a stop to ... Dear God, what misguided men ... that Papanastasias ... and Papadianos ... They aren't holy pictures but idols, accursed idols,' exclaimed Nikeforos, gesticulating with his twisted hands. 'Idols ... idols ... idols ...'

(1936)

Brother Francis

ON the road to Forli, where the way turns off to Lugo, a begging friar stopped at a blacksmith's forge. He was a small, rather shrunken figure and showed his yellow teeth in a wide smile.

'God give you good morrow, brother smith,' he said cheerily, 'I have not broken my fast this day.'

The smith straightened himself up, wiped away the sweat and murmured something to himself about loafers and vagabonds.

'Come in,' he grunted. 'There'll be a piece of cheese within.'

The smith's wife was with child. She was a pious woman and would have kissed the friar's hand, but he swiftly tucked both hands away and babbled brightly:

'But, little mother, what if I should kiss *your* hand? They call me Brother Francis the beggar. God's blessing on you.'

'Amen,' sighed the smith's young wife, and went for bread, cheese and wine.

The smith was a man of few words. He looked at the ground and could think of nothing to say. 'And where do you come from, Father?' he asked at last.

'From Assisi,' said the friar. 'A good step, that, brother. You'd never believe what the world holds of streams, vineyards and footpaths. One cannot go and look at them all, yet we should, brother, we should. Everywhere is the work of God's hand, and as you walk along 'tis as if you were praying.'

'I went as far as Bologna once,' remarked the smith thoughtfully, 'but that's a long time ago. You know, Father, a smith can't carry his forge about with him.'

The friar nodded. 'To work iron,' he said, 'there's a way of serving God! The fire is fair and holy. Why, brother, fire is a living creature of God. When the iron grows soft and you can bend it – how beautiful that is, brother smith! And when you look into the fire – 'tis like having a revelation.' The friar clasped his hands round his knees like a boy and began to talk about fire. The shepherds' fires, the smoky little fires in the vineyards, the flaming pinewood torch and the burning bush. In the meantime the smith's wife spread the table with a white linen cloth and set out bread, cheese and wine; the smith blinked as if he were looking into a fire.

'Father,' said the woman softly, 'do you not care to eat?'

Brother Francis broke the bread in his fingers and looked questioningly at the smith and his wife. What is amiss with you two, he wondered, why are you so silent and dejected? Such good people, the man as strong as iron and the woman blessed, what ails you, then, what afflicts you? The morsels in his mouth grew big with his perplexity and pity. How shall I cheer you, God's children that you are? Shall I tell you merry jests from my journeyings? Shall I sing and leap to rejoice the heart of the woman who is waiting?

The door opened a little. The woman raised her hand and turned pale. In the doorway appeared a dog's head, submissive and with eyes full of fear.

The smith sprang up, the veins on his forehead distended with blood, and rushed to the door. 'Get out, you cursed hound,' he roared, and kicked the door. The dog whimpered and ran away.

Brother Francis looked distressed and rolled his bread perplexedly into balls. 'Brother smith, brother smith,' he caught him up, 'what has God's creature there done to you?'

The smith turned anxiously to his wife. 'There, there, Giuliana,' he said gruffly, 'there, there.'

The woman tried to smile, but her lips trembled; she stood up, pale and shaking, and went out without a word. The smith stared after her sombrely.

'Little brother,' whispered Francis sorrowfully, 'why do you drive your brother dog from the table? If there is not enough for all, let me go.'

The smith cleared his throat angrily. 'Well, if you want to know, Father,' he said harshly, 'that dog ... At Easter we were expecting a visitor. My wife's little sister was to come to us from Forli ... She never came. A fortnight later her parents came to fetch her ... We hunted high and low for the child, there was no trace of her anywhere. Then a week before Pentecost, our dog came running in from somewhere in the fields, dragging something in his mouth on to the threshold. We looked to see what it was – entrails. It was only then that we found what was left of the little girl ...' The smith bit his lip to control himself. 'We don't know who did it. God will punish the murderer. But that dog, Father ...' The smith waved his hand. 'I can't kill him, that's the worst of all. And he won't be driven away. He hangs about round the house and begs ... You can understand, Father, how frightful ...' The smith kneaded his face with a horny hand. 'We can't bear the sight of him. At night he whines at the door ...'

Brother Francis shuddered.

'That's how it is,' growled the smith. 'Forgive me, Father, I must look to Giuliana.'

The friar was left alone in the room; the silence was so complete that he felt uncomfortable. He went on tip-toe to the porch. Standing a little apart was a shivering yellow dog with its tail between its legs, who raised its eyes to him uncertainly. Brother Francis turned towards him. The dog wagged its tail tentatively and whined.

'Alas, poor creature,' murmured Francis, and tried to look away from it, but the dog wagged its tail and did not take its eyes from him. 'There, there, what d'you want?' grunted Francis in perplexity. 'You're sad, little brother, aren't you? It's a sad business.' The dog shifted from one paw to another and trembled with emotion. 'There, there,' said Francis caressingly. 'Will no one talk to you?' The dog whimpered and crawled to the friar's feet. Brother Francis felt somehow nauseated by him. 'Go, go away,' he said earnestly. 'You shouldn't have done it, little brother. It was the holy flesh of a little girl ...' The dog lay at the saint's feet and whimpered. 'Stop, I beg you,' grumbled Francis, and bent over the dog. The dog stiffened with extreme expectation.

At that moment the smith and his wife came to the threshold, for they were looking for their guest. And lo the friar was kneeling before the house scratching the sobbing dog behind the ear and saying softly: 'There, there, little brother, there, there, my dear. What, do you want to lick my hand?'

The smith snorted. Francis turned to him and said timidly: 'He did beg so, brother! What is his name? What do you call him?'

'Bracco,' growled the smith.

'Bracco,' said Saint Francis, and the dog quickly licked

his face. Francis rose. 'Enough, brother, I thank you. I must be going, brother smith.' He did not know for the moment how to take his leave. He stood before the black-smith's wife with half-closed eyes, thinking of a blessing.

When he opened his eyes the young woman was kneel-ing before him and she had placed her hand on the head of the yellow dog. 'Praise God,' sighed Francis and showed his yellow teeth. 'God reward you, little sister.'

And the dog, yelping with frantic delight, began to scamper in circles round the Saint and the kneeling woman.

Ophir

THE folk in the Piazza di San Marco looked round curiously as the sbirri led the old man to the Doge's palace. He was exhausted and very dirty; he looked like some low rascal from the port.

'This man,' said the *podestà vicegerente*, standing before the Doge's throne, 'says that he is Giovanni Fialho, a merchant from Lisbon; he asserts that he was the owner of a ship which the Algerian pirates captured from him with her whole crew and cargo; he alleges that he managed to escape from the galleys and that he can do great service to the Republic of Venice – but what this service is he will only tell to yourself, Messer Doge.'

The venerable Doge looked attentively at the scrubby little old sailor with his birdlike eyes. 'So,' he said at last, 'you say that you worked in the galleys?'

Instead of answering the man bared his dirty ankles; they were swollen from wearing manacles. 'And my back, Your Magnificence, is covered with scars. If you would like me to show them –'

'No, no,' said the Doge hurriedly. 'There is no need. What did you wish to say to us?'

The wretched man raised his head. 'Give me a ship, Your Magnificence,' he said in a clear voice. 'I'll sail her to Ophir, the land of gold.'

'To Ophir,' murmured the Doge. 'You have found Ophir?'

'I have,' said the old man, 'and I stayed there nine months, for we had to repair the ship.'

The Doge exchanged a quick glance with his learned adviser, the Bishop of Pordenone. 'Where is Ophir?' he asked the old seaman.

'Three months' voyage from here,' said the man. 'You must sail all round Africa and then you must sail northwards again.'

The Bishop of Pordenone bent his head attentively. 'And is Ophir on the sea coast?'

'No, Monsignore. It is nine days' journey from the seashore and it stretches all round a great lake as blue as sapphire.'

The Bishop of Pordenone nodded his head slightly.

'And how did you reach the interior of the land?' asked the Doge. 'They say that Ophir is separated from the sea by impenetrable mountains and deserts.'

'It is true,' said Fialho, 'no road leads to Ophir. The desert swarms with lions and the mountains are as smooth and polished as Murano glass.'

'And you have been beyond them?' asked the Doge.

'I have. While we were repairing our ship, which had been badly damaged by storms, some men clad in white robes edged with purple came down to the beach and beckoned to us.'

'Negroes?' asked the Bishop.

'No, Monsignore. As white as the English and with long hair sprinkled with golden powder. They were very handsome.'

'And were they armed?' asked the Doge.

'They had golden daggers. They bade us bring everything we had that was made of iron, and in Ophir they would exchange it for gold; for in Ophir there is no iron. They saw to it that we collected all the iron we had:

anchors, chains, swords, even the nails with which we were repairing the ship.'

'And what next?' asked the Doge.

'A herd of winged mules was waiting on the shore – about seventy of them. They had wings like swans. They are called *pegasi*.'

'*Pegasi*,' said the learned bishop thoughtfully. 'Reports of such beasts have come down to us from the ancient Greeks. It seems, then, that the Greeks actually knew Ophir.'

'They speak Greek in Ophir,' declared the old seaman. 'I know a little Greek, because in every port there's always some scoundrel from Crete or Smyrna.'

'This is interesting information,' grunted the bishop. 'And are the people of Ophir Christians?'

'May God pardon me,' said Fialho, 'but they are as heathen as logs of wood, Monsignore. They worship a certain Apollo, or whatever they call him.'

The Bishop of Pordenone nodded his head. 'That all fits in. They will be the descendants of the Greeks who were scattered by the storm after the fall of Troy. And what more?'

'What more?' said Giovanni Fialho. 'We loaded the iron upon the winged mules. Three of us, myself, a certain Chico of Cadiz and Manolo Pereira of Coimbra, were given winged horses, and guided by these men of Ophir we flew due eastwards. The journey lasted nine days. We dismounted each night for the *pegasi* to feed and drink. They eat nothing but asphodels and narcissi.'

'Clearly they are of Greek origin,' murmured the bishop.

'On the ninth day we caught sight of a lake as blue as sapphire,' the old seaman went on. 'We dismounted on its shore. There are silver fish in it with ruby eyes. And the sand of this lake, Your Magnificence, is all of pearls as big as grains of wheat. Manolo threw himself on the ground and plunged his arms elbow deep in the pearls; and then one of our guides told us that it is an excellent sand and that in Ophir they burn it down for lime.'

The Doge rolled his eyes. 'Lime made from pearls! That is astounding!'

'Then they led us to the royal palace. All of alabaster, it was, only the roof was of gold, and it shone like the sun. There we were received by the Queen of Ophir, sitting upon a crystal throne.'

'What, does a woman rule in Ophir?' asked the bishop, amazed.

'Thus it is, Monsignore. A woman of dazzling beauty, like a goddess.'

'Of course, one of the Amazons,' said the bishop thoughtfully.

'And what about the other women?' asked the Doge. 'I mean the women in general. Are they good looking?'

The sailor clasped his hands. 'Ah, Your Magnificence, I've never seen such women! Not even in Lisbon in my young days!'

The Doge waved an impatient hand. 'Tut, tut! In Lisbon, they say, the women are the colour of black cats. But in Venice, my man, in Venice some thirty years ago, what women there used to be then! Like Titian's paintings! And what about these women of Ophir? Tell us.'

'I'm an old man, Your Magnificence,' said Fialho, 'but Manolo would have been able to tell you if he hadn't been killed by the Mussulmans who captured us off the Balearic islands.'

'Could he have told us much?' asked the Doge with interest.

'Mother of God!' cried the old sailor, 'Your Magnificence wouldn't have believed it all! I tell you, when we'd been there a fortnight he was as thin as a rake.'

'And what about the Queen?'

'The Queen wore an iron girdle and iron bracelets. "They tell me you have some iron," she said. "The Arab merchants sometimes bring iron here." '

'The Arab merchants!' shouted the Doge and brought his fist down on the arm of his chair. 'There you see, the scoundrels are snapping up our markets on all sides! It is not to be endured. This is a matter touching the political prestige of the Republic of Venice! I will give you three ships, Giovanni, three shiploads of iron –'

The bishop raised his hand. 'And what more, Giovanni?'

'The Queen offered to take all my iron in exchange for an equal weight of gold.'

'And of course you accepted, you robber!'

'No, Monsignore. I told her that I did not sell iron by weight but by bulk.'

'True,' said the bishop. 'Gold is heavier.'

'Especially the gold of Ophir, Monsignore. It is three times as heavy as ordinary gold and as red as fire. So the Queen gave orders for them to forge from gold an anchor, nails, chains and weapons exactly like our iron ones. That was why we had to stay there for some weeks.'

'And what do they need iron for?' asked the Doge curiously.

'Because it is rare, Your Magnificence,' said the old merchant. 'They make it into jewellery and money. They hoard iron nails in coffers as treasures. They say that iron is more beautiful than gold.'

The Doge blinked his eyelids, which were like a turkey's. 'Remarkable,' he grunted. 'This is most remarkable, Giovanni. And what happened after that?'

'They loaded all the gold on to the winged mules and

took us back to the seashore the way we had come. There we hammered the golden nails into our ship and hung the golden anchor on golden chains. The tattered rigging and sails we replaced with silken ones, and we sailed away with a fair breeze towards our native land.'

'And what about the pearls?' asked the Doge. 'Did you not bring any of the pearls away with yoou?'

'We did not,' said Fialho. 'Your Magnificence will pardon me, but they were as common as sand. A few grains did get stuck in our shoes, and even those were taken from us by the Algerian infidels when they fell upon us off the Balearic islands.'

'It appears,' murmured the Doge, 'that this description has considerable verisimilitude.'

The bishop gave a little sign of assent. 'And what about the animals?' he asked as an afterthought. 'Are there any centaurs in Ophir?'

'I did not hear of them, Monsignore,' replied the sailor respectfully, 'but there are flamingoes.'

The bishop gave a snort. 'You must be mistaken. Flamingoes live in Egypt – it is known that they have only one leg.'

'And they have wild asses there,' added the sailor, 'which are striped black and white after the manner of a tiger.'

The bishop looked up suspiciously. 'Don't try to fool us, Giovanni. Who ever saw striped asses? There is one thing which surprises me. You allege that you flew over the mountains of Ophir on winged mules.'

'So it was, Monsignore.'

'Now, let us see. According to the reports of the Arabs, there is in the mountains of Ophir a bird called the Noh which, as we know, has a steel beak, steel claws and bronze pinions. Did you hear nothing of this bird?'

'No, Monsignore, I did not,' stammered the seaman.

The Bishop of Pordenone shook his head thoughtfully. 'You could not have flown across those mountains, man, you will never persuade us of that. It has been proved that this bird lives there. Thus it is technically impossible that you should have flown across. The Noh would have snapped you up as a swallow snaps up flies. You can't take us in like that. And what about the trees, you trickster?'

'Why as for the trees,' burst from the unhappy man, 'it's known what kind they are. Palms, Monsignore.'

'There, you see you are lying!' cried the bishop triumphantly. 'According to Bubon of Biskra, who is an authority in these matters, there are pomegranate trees in Ophir, and the fruit they bear has carbuncles instead of seeds. It's a silly story you've invented, my man.'

Giovanni Fialho fell on his knees. 'As God's above me, Monsignore, how could an unlettered seaman like me invent Ophir?'

'Don't try to teach me,' the bishop rebuked him, 'I know better than you that there is such a place as Ophir, the land of gold. But as for you, you're a liar and a knave. What you tell us is refuted by reliable authorities, therefore it must be false. Messer Doge, this man is an impostor.'

'Another of them?' sighed the aged Doge, blinking uneasily. 'It is terrible how many of these adventurers there are nowadays. Take him away.'

The *podestà vicegerente* glanced at him questioningly.

'The same as usual, the same as usual,' yawned the Doge. 'Let him sit in prison till he's blue and then sell him to the galleys. It's a pity,' he grumbled, 'that he's an impostor; some of what he said seemed to have a kernel of truth in it ... Perhaps he heard it from the Arabs.'

(1932)

Goneril

No, nothing's the matter with me, nurse – and don't call me your little pretty one. I know you called me that when I was little; and King Lear called me a young rapscallion, didn't he? He would rather have had a son. Do you think boys are really nicer than girls? Regan was always so ladylike, and Cordelia – you know – so absent-minded. A regular butter-fingers. And Regan – there was no saying a word to her; nose in the air like a queen, but selfish, do you remember? She always had it in her. Tell me, nurse, was I bad when I was little? There, you see !

How does one begin to turn wicked? I *know* I'm wicked, nurse. Don't say I'm not; you think so too. I don't mind what you all think of me. Even if you think me wicked. But over that business with father I was in the right, nurse. Why on earth did he get the idea that he must take those hundred fellows of his about with him? and if there had only been a hundred of them, but there were all sorts of rag, tag and bobtail besides – it simply wouldn't do. I'd have liked to have him, nurse, truly I would; I was fond of him, terribly fond, fonder than of anyone else in the world; but those followers of his, my God ! – They simply made a bear-garden of the place ! Just remember, nurse, what it looked like: full of loafers, nothing but brawls and quarrelling and shouting, and the dirt, well – Worse than a dunghill. Tell me, nurse, would any mistress of a household have put up with *that*? And I couldn't give them orders – oh no ! Only King Lear was allowed to order them about. They just made faces at me. At night they went after the maids – I kept on hearing tapping and rustling and whistling – the duke slept like a log; I used to wake him and say, can't you hear? And he just grunted, leave them alone, and went off to sleep again. Just think what it was like for *me*, nurse, while that was going on! You have been young yourself, you can understand. When I complained to King Lear he just laughed at me: Why, my girl, what else can you expect of the fellows? Stop up your ears and don't think about it.

And so I told him that it wouldn't do, that he must send away at least half of the lazy fellows who were eating me out of house and home. And as you know, he was insulted. He called it ingratitude and I don't know what besides. You've no idea what a rage he flew into. And yet I know what can be done and what can't. Men only bother about their honour, but we women have to think about running the house in an orderly way. *They* don't care if it's an absolute pigsty. Tell me, nurse, was I right or not? There, you see! And father took it as a deadly insult. What was I to do? I know my duty to him, but as a woman I have a duty to my home, haven't I? And so father cursed me. And the duke – he just stood there, blinking and shifting from one foot to the other. D'you think he stood up for me? No. He let me be treated like a wicked, mean, scolding woman. Listen, nurse, at that moment something seemed to snap inside me: I – I – I began to *hate* my husband. I hate him. There, now you know! *I hate him!* And I hate my father because it's his fault, do you understand? So there you are; I'm wicked, I know, but I'm only wicked because I was in the right –

No, don't say anything; I am really wicked. You know I have a lover, don't you? If you only realized how little I mind your knowing! Do you think I love Edmund? I don't; but I want to be revenged on the duke because he didn't behave like a man. I simply hate him. Nurse, you can't imagine what it is to hate! It means to be bad, bad, bad through and through! When one begins to hate – one seems to change altogether. I used to be quite a good girl, nurse, and I might have grown into a good woman; I used to be a daughter, I used to be a sister, and now I am only wicked. Now I don't love even you, nurse, I don't love even myself – I was in the right; if they had admitted that, I should be a different woman, believe me –

No, I'm not crying. Don't think it makes me sad. Not a bit. One is freer when one hates. One can think what one likes – one needn't stop at anything. You know, *before* I hadn't the courage to see my husband as he is, to see that he is disagreeable and fat and a coward and that his hands are damp; and now I see it. Now I see that my father Lear is a ridiculous tyrant, that he's a toothless and muddle-headed old man – I see everything. I see that Regan is a viper and that I – Oh, nurse, I have such strange and terrible things in me – I used not to have any idea of it before. It happened all of a sudden. Tell me, is it *my* fault? I was in the right; they shouldn't have driven me so far …

You can't understand it, nurse. Sometimes I feel as if I could kill the duke when he's snoring beside me. Just stick a sword into him. Or poison Regan. Here's a cup of wine for you, sister, drink it up. Did you know that Regan is trying to get Edmund away from me? Not because she loves him; Regan's as cold as a stone. She's just doing it to spite me. And she counts on Edmund clearing that blockhead of a duke out of his way somehow and seizing the throne after Lear's death. I know that's how it is, nurse. Regan's a widow now – she always had luck, the cat. But you needn't think she'll be successful: I'm on the watch and I hate them all. I don't even sleep, I just lie awake thinking and hating. If you only knew how beautifully and boundlessly one can hate in the darkness. And when I remember that it all came about just through father's obstinacy and the mess they made in the house. You must admit no lady could have put up with it . . .

Nurse, nurse, nurse, why didn't they see all that time ago that I was in the right?

(1933)

Hamlet, Prince of Denmark

SCENE X

(Rosencrantz and Guildenstern are going out.)

HAMLET: One moment, dear Guildenstern; a word, Rosencrantz!

ROSENCRANTZ: At your service, prince.

GUILDENSTERN: What is your wish, prince?

HAMLET: Just a question. How would you say the court performance of that tragedy about the man who poisoned a king affected the King?

ROSENCRANTZ: Terribly, prince.

HAMLET: Really terribly?

GUILDENSTERN: The King was beside himself.

HAMLET: And the Queen?

ROSENCRANTZ: The Queen fainted.

HAMLET: And the others?

GUILDENSTERN: Whom does Your Highness mean?

HAMLET: Well, you and the courtiers and the court ladies and everyone who was in the hall while the play was going on. Didn't they say anything?

ROSENCRANTZ: Nothing, prince.

GUILDENSTERN: They were too much impressed to say a word.

HAMLET: What about Polonius?

GUILDENSTERN: Polonius wept.

HAMLET: And the courtiers?

ROSENCRANTZ: The courtiers sobbed. I myself, prince,

could not restrain my tears and I saw how friend
Guildenstern hid the tell-tale moisture in his eyes with
his sleeve.

HAMLET: And the soldiers?

GUILDENSTERN: They turned their faces away to conceal their profound emotion.

HAMLET: Then you think the play was –

ROSENCRANTZ: A tremendous success.

GUILDENSTERN: But a deserved one.

ROSENCRANTZ: Such magnificent scenery!

GUILDENSTERN: And such a thrilling plot!

HAMLET: Hm, I should have said that the play had its
faults –

ROSENCRANTZ: Your pardon, prince, what faults?

HAMLET: For instance ... I think it could have been
better acted. I know those actors did their best, but their
king wasn't kingly enough or their murderer murderous
enough. Dear sirs, if I'd been that murderer then, by
Hecate, even a murderer would have seen for the first
time what murder is! Judge for yourselves! (*He acts.*)

ROSENCRANTZ: Simply marvellous, prince!

GUILDENSTERN: Brilliantly acted!

ROSENCRANTZ: By heaven, anyone would say that you
had seen a murderer slinking along to do his monstrous
work.

HAMLET: No, Rosencrantz, it's just in me – where from
and why? Who knows? Pst, come nearer. Hamlet –

GUILDENSTERN: What, prince?

HAMLET: – has his secret.

ROSENCRANTZ: Really, prince?

HAMLET: A great secret. Not for the courtiers but for
the ears of my best friends. Come close!

GUILDENSTERN: Yes, prince.

HAMLET: No, not prince!

GUILDENSTERN: No, Your Highness.

HAMLET: Just Hamlet.

GUILDENSTERN: As you wish, prince.

HAMLET: Now listen, and keep my plan, which I have carefully thought over, to yourselves.

ROSENCRANTZ: What plan, dear prince?

HAMLET: I want to be an actor.

ROSENCRANTZ: Really, prince?

HAMLET: It is decided, Rosencrantz. Tomorrow I want to go out into the world with these actors. In one town after another they will act this play about the great king who was murdered; about the murderer who succeeded to his throne and to his marriage bed almost before it had grown cold; and about the queen who, a bare month a widow, lay dallying on the sweaty, greasy bed with the murderer and coward, the scoundrel, the criminal who stole the kingdom ... The more I think about it the more his figure attracts me. To act him in all his vileness, the base, degenerate reptile who infects everything that he touches with the plague – what a part! Only it would have to be acted differently from that strolling player – he did what he could but he could not rise to such heights of evil. Let him play the king; he isn't great enough for the villain. The part was thrown away on him. How I would have acted it, how I would have got inside his slippery soul until I had squeezed all human wickedness out of it to the last drop. What a part!

GUILDENSTERN: And what a play!

HAMLET: The play wasn't altogether bad –

ROSENCRANTZ: It was first-rate!

HAMLET: Some of the details could have been better worked out – I may possibly come back to the subject later – it would be worth it; that treacherous king, that monstrous, base, abominable character attracts me enormously. Dear Rosencrantz, I want to write plays.

ROSENCRANTZ: Simply marvellous, prince!

HAMLET: Write – I shall write. I've got so many subjects already – that villain was the first. The second will be about the cringing, mean-spirited courtiers –

ROSENCRANTZ: Top hole, prince!

HAMLET: The third, a comedy about a stupid old chamberlain –

GUILDENSTERN: A first-rate subject!

HAMLET: The fourth will be a play about a girl.

ROSENCRANTZ: What sort of play?

HAMLET: Oh, just a play.

GUILDENSTERN: A most promising subject!

ROSENCRANTZ: Quite poetic.

HAMLET: And Hamlet will write. On the throne a villain will grind the faces of the defenceless people, the courtiers will bend their backs, and Hamlet will write. And there will be wars, things will grow worse for the weak and better for the strong, and Hamlet will write. So as not to rise and do something –

GUILDENSTERN: What, prince?

HAMLET: How should I know? What does one do against a bad government?

ROSENCRANTZ: Nothing, prince.

HAMLET: Nothing at all?

GUILDENSTERN: Well, in the history books you sometimes find men who place themselves at the head of the people and urge them by their eloquence or their example to rise against the bad government and smash it.

ROSENCRANTZ: But that, prince, is only done in history books.

HAMLET: Well, well. Only in the history books. And you say that eloquence can stir the people up? Affliction is dumb. Someone must come who will call a spade a spade and say: Look here, this is oppression, this is injustice, an infamous crime has been perpetrated against you all and the man who calls himself your king is a criminal, a cheat, a murderer and an adulterer – that's a fact, isn't it? If you are men at all why do you put up with this sea of trouble, why don't you snatch up swords and clubs? or are you quite unmanned by shame? are you slaves who can bear to live without honour –?

GUILDENSTERN: You are eloquent, prince.

HAMLET: Eloquent, you say? What if I came forward like the man in the history books and made my eloquence the voice of the people?

ROSENCRANTZ: The people are certainly devoted to their prince.

HAMLET: And then at their head overthrew the infected throne?

GUILDENSTERN: Your pardon, prince, but that's politics.

HAMLET: It's an odd feeling to see such a great task before one ! Thanks, gentlemen.

ROSENCRANTZ: We will not disturb your Highness further.

(*Exeunt* Rosencrantz *and* Guildenstern)

HAMLET: To be or not to be, that is the question. And if to be, then what? Oh heavens ! To be a prince. To stand beside the throne with a smile on my lips, courteous, loyal – and why not on the throne? No, another is there. Then merely to wait till he dies, till the black blood curdles in his veins ! Must I? No ! Rather plunge a knife into the traitor's breast and avenge my father's death ! Wash the disgrace from my mother's bed ! Why do I still hesitate? Am I a bloodless coward, or what? No, that's not it. My eyes drink in his loathsome face, his lascivious lips and ogling eyes and I feel: now I've got him, now I could do him exactly! and secretly I try to put on the expression of his bestial jowl. What a part! To be an actor, yes; I'd show up all the hidden, shameless evil lurking in the smiling villain – it's fascinating, fascinating. But would the face be recognized only by his contemporaries – and no one else besides? – Rather convict him for ever and all the human monsters and all the rottenness with which he surrounded himself in the state of Denmark! What a splendid task! – But I am a poet! Then I can set down an indictment which will outlast the ages and, with an imperishable finger, point to the festering sore – Why, what eloquence! Isn't it waste to squander it all on myself? Why not stand up in the market-place, summon the people and talk and talk – They are not made of clay; an eloquent man can make them pull themselves together and stir up a cleansing storm against all tyrants! It's fascinating, fascinating. But then I couldn't act him! What waste! What an actor I could be! But if I were an actor, could I unleash the storm which brings thrones thundering down? – But then again I couldn't write my other plays! What waste! – Well then, what? Am I to unmask him by acting on the stage, or to nail him to the gates for ages like a bat, or sweep him from the throne with the enraged people? What, then, what? – And supposing I persuade myself that I want to be revenged? Why be an actor only to tear the mask from his jowl? If I'm to act, it is because acting is in me and I must – I must create human characters, whether they be good or base! I should love to act him – what a part! – To be simply an actor! Or just to write, not for revenge but simply for the joy of having words come to life under my hand – And why only write? Why not rather talk? Be an orator, be a leader of the people and talk, talk as a bird sings, so beautifully and so captivatingly that I should convince myself and believe what I said! – That's it. Be wholly something, that is the saving word! Be an actor. Or write? Or go with the people? This or that! Oh hell! Which shall I choose? What shall Hamlet do? What I could do if I were only something! – Yes, but what? That is the question!

(1934)

Don Juan's Confession

THE death of the unhappy Doña Elvira had been avenged; Don Juan Tenorio lay with a sword-thrust through his chest in the Posada de las Reinas, obviously at the point of death.

'Emphysema of the lungs,' grunted the local doctor. 'Some people might recover from it, but a caballero so worn out by debauchery as Don Juan – These are difficult matters, Leporello; I may tell you I don't like his heart. Well, it's to be understood: after such excesses *in venere* – it is a well-explained asthenic case, gentlemen. To be on the safe side, Leporello, I'd send for a priest; he may come to himself again, though in the present-day state of science – I don't know. I have the honour to take my leave of you, caballeros.'

Thus it happened that Padre Jacinto sat at the foot of Don Juan's bed and waited for the patient to come to from his swoon; in the meantime he prayed for his notoriously sinful soul. If I could only save this lost sinner, bound for hell, thought the good father; he seems to be really finished – perhaps that will humble his pride and bring his mind to a state of repentant sorrow. It isn't everyone who gets hold of such a famous and unscrupulous profligate; why, perhaps even the Bishop of Burgos hasn't had such a notorious case. People will whisper: Look, that's Padre Jacinto, the man who saved Don Juan's soul –

He started and crossed himself, partly because he had recovered from the devilish temptation of pride, partly because he realized that the burning and slightly mocking eyes of the dying Don Juan were fixed upon him.

'My dear son,' said the reverend Padre as kindly as he could, 'you are dying; in a little while you will stand before God's judgement seat, burdened with all the sins which you have committed in your dissolute life. I beg you, for the love of our Lord, to confess them while you have time; it is not fitting that you should make your pilgrimage into the other world clothed in the garment of your wickedness and smirched with the filth of your worldly offences.'

'Yes,' murmured Don Juan. 'I must change my clothes again. Padre, I have always made a point of dressing suitably for the occasion.'

'I am afraid,' said Padre Jacinto, 'that you do not altogether understand me. I am asking you if you wish to confess your sins and repent.'

'Confess?' repeated Don Juan weakly. 'Blacken myself thoroughly. Ah, Father, you wouldn't believe what an impression it makes on women.'

'Juan,' said the good father sternly, 'put these worldly thoughts from you; remember that you have to speak with your Creator.'

'I know,' said Don Juan courteously. 'And I know it's the proper thing to die like a Christian. I've always been careful to do the proper thing – as far as possible, Father. On my honour, I'll tell you everything straight out without mincing matters; in the first place I'm too weak for long speeches and in the second place it's always been my principle to go straight to the point without beating about the bush.'

'I applaud your submission,' said Father Jacinto. 'But first of all, my dear son, prepare yourself thoroughly, examine your conscience and awaken in yourself humble repentance for your wrongdoings. I will wait.'

Don Juan closed his eyes and examined his conscience while the priest prayed silently for help and enlightenment from God.

'I'm ready, Father,' said Don Juan after a time and began his confession. Padre Jacinto nodded his head in satisfaction; it seemed to be a frank and full confession; it did not leave out either lies or blasphemy, murder, perjury, pride, deceit or treachery – Don Juan was truly a grievous sinner. And suddenly he stopped as if exhausted and closed his eyes.

'Rest a little, my dear son,' the priest encouraged him patiently, 'and then continue.'

'I've finished, reverend Father,' said Don Juan. 'If I've forgotten anything it's certainly only details which God will be kind enough to forgive me.'

'What?' cried Father Jacinto, 'do you call them details? What about the lasciviousness in which you have wallowed all your life? What about the women whom you have seduced? What about the unchaste passions which you have followed in an unbridled manner? Confess yourself properly, my son; not one of your shameless actions is hidden from God, you unprincipled man; you had better repent of your wickedness and unburden your sinful soul!'

A painful and impatient expression appeared on Don Juan's face. 'I've told you already, Father,' he said obstinately. 'I've finished. On my honour, I've nothing more to tell you.'

Just then the innkeeper of the Posada de las Reinas heard a roar from the room of the wounded man. 'God defend us!' he cried and crossed himself, 'Padre Jacinto seems to be casting the devil out of the poor gentleman.

Oh Lord, I don't really like goings on like this in my inn !'

The roaring lasted a good time, about as long as you would boil beans; at times it sank to earnest exhortation, at times it broke out in wild clamour; suddenly Padre Jacinto, red as a turkey cock and calling on the Mother of God, burst out of the wounded gentleman's room and rushed into the church. After that there was silence in the inn; only the sorrowful Leporello crept into the room where his master lay with closed eyes, groaning.

*

That afternoon Padre Ildefonso of the Society of Jesus arrived in the town; he was travelling on mule-back from Madrid to Burgos, and because it was a very hot day he dismounted at the priest's house and visited Father Jacinto. He was a gaunt priest, as dried up as an old smoked sausage and with bristling eyebrows like the armpits of an old cavalryman.

When they had drunk a cup of sour milk together, he fixed his eyes on Father Jacinto, who tried in vain to hide that something was troubling him. It was so quiet that the buzzing of the flies seemed almost thunderous.

'Well you see, it's like this,' the worried Padre Jacinto burst out at last. 'I have a grievous sinner here who is lying *in extremis*. In fact, Don Ildefonso, it is the wretched Don Juan Tenorio. He had an intrigue or a duel here, or something – anyway, I came to confess him. At first everything went swimmingly; he made a very proper confession, saying only what was true; but when we got to the seventh commandment – nothing. I couldn't get a word out of him. He said he hadn't anything to tell me. Mother of God, the scoundrel ! When I consider that he is the worst profligate in the two Castiles – they say there is not his equal even in Valencia or Cadiz. They say that in the last few years he has seduced six hundred and ninety-seven young women; a hundred and thirteen of them went into nunneries, about fifty were killed by their fathers or husbands in righteous wrath and about the same number died of grief. And now just imagine, Don Ildefonso, this libertine withstands me to the face on his death-bed that *in puncto fornicationis* he has nothing to confess! What do you say to that?'

'Nothing,' said the Jesuit father. 'And you refused him absolution?'

'Of course I did,' answered Padre Jacinto dejectedly. 'Nothing I said was any good. I admonished him till I should have awakened repentance in a stone, but it had absolutely no effect on this arch-reprobate. "I may have sinned through pride, father," he said to me, "I have broken my oath, anything you like; but in the matter about which you ask, I have nothing to say." And do you know what that means, Don Ildefonso?' Father Jacinto burst out suddenly and crossed himself with a trembling hand. 'I think he was in league with the devil. That is why he cannot confess it. It was an unclean enchantment. He seduced women by diabolical power.' Father Jacinto shuddered. 'You might have a look at him, Domine. In my opinion the thing looks out of his eyes.'

Don Ildefonso, S.J., considered in silence. 'If you think so,' he said at last, 'I will go and see this man.'

*

Don Juan was dozing when Don Ildefonso stepped softly into the room and dismissed Leporello with a movement of his hand; then he sat down on a chair at the head of the bed and studied the hollow-cheeked face of the dying man.

After a very long time the wounded man moaned and opened his eyes.

'Don Juan,' said the Jesuit gently, 'I think it would exhaust you to talk.'

Don Juan nodded weakly.

'It doesn't matter,' said the Jesuit. 'Your confession, Don Juan, was not clear on one point. I am not going to ask you questions, but perhaps you could indicate whether you agree or disagree with what I am going to say – about you.'

The wounded man fixed his eyes almost in anguish on the motionless face of the priest.

'Don Juan,' began Don Ildefonso almost lightly, 'I have heard about you for a long time; I have pondered upon the real reason why you rush headlong from one woman to another, from one love affair to another; why you can never pause, never stop in that fulfilment and peace which we men call happiness –'

Don Juan showed his teeth in a grimace of pain.

'From one love affair to another,' Don Ildefonso went on quietly. 'As though you kept on trying over and over again to convince someone – obviously yourself – that *you are capable of love, that you are the kind of man whom women love* – poor Don Juan !'

The wounded man's lips moved; it was as though he were repeating the last words.

'And all the time,' the priest went on in a friendly voice, 'you have never been a man, Don Juan; only your spirit was the spirit of a man and it was ashamed, señor, and tried desperately to hide the fact that nature had not given you what is given to every living creature –'

A boyish moan sounded from the bed.

'And so, Don Juan, *you have played at being a man* ever since your adolescence; you have been recklessly brave, adventurous, proud and ostentatious so as to drown the humiliating feeling within you that others were better and more virile than you; but it was a lie and so you went on extravagantly heaping proof upon proof; none could satisfy you because it was only a barren pretence – you have never seduced even one woman, Don Juan. You have never known what it is to love, you have only striven feverishly whenever you met a desirable and well-born woman to bewitch her by your spirit, your chivalry, your passion, of which you convinced yourself by your own eloquence; all this you could do perfectly, because *you acted* it. And when the moment came when a woman's knees gave way beneath her – it must have been hell for you, Don Juan, it must have been hell because in that moment you experienced your accursed pride and at the same time your most terrible humiliation. And you had to tear yourself from the embrace which you had conquered at the risk of your life and run, poor Don Juan, run away from the arms of the woman you had won, run away with some fine lie on those irresistible lips. It must have been hell, Don Juan.'

The wounded man turned his face to the wall and wept.

Don Ildefonso stood up. 'Poor boy,' he said, 'you were ashamed to admit it even in your holy confession. Well, well, it is all over now, but I must not deprive Father Jacinto of his penitent.'

He sent for the priest; and when Father Jacinto came Don Ildefonso said to him: 'See, Father, he has admitted everything and has wept. His repentance is humble beyond all doubt; I think we might give him absolution.'

(1932)

Romeo and Juliet

A YOUNG English gentleman, Oliver Mendeville, who was making the grand tour in Italy, received news in Florence that his father, Sir William, had departed this life. Sir Oliver therefore bade farewell with a heavy heart and many tears to Signorina Maddalena, promising to come back as soon as he could, and set out with his servant on the road to Genoa.

On the third day of their journey they were overtaken by a heavy downpour of rain just as they were riding into a poor and scattered hamlet. Sir Oliver halted his horse under an ancient elm.

'Paolo,' he said to his servant, 'find if there is an *albergo* here where we can shelter till the storm has passed.'

'For your servant and horses,' said a voice above his head, 'the inn is yonder round the bend in the road. But you, *cavaliere*, would do great honour to my house if you would shelter beneath its humble roof.'

Sir Oliver doffed his broad-brimmed hat and looked up at the window from which a fat old priest was smiling merrily down at him.

'*Vossignoria reverendissima*,' he said politely, 'you show too much kindness to a stranger who is leaving your lovely country with a heavy debt of gratitude for all the goodness which has been heaped upon him so bounteously.'

'*Bene*, dear son,' answered the priest, 'but if you go on talking a moment longer you will be wet to the skin. Be good enough to dismount from your horse and give your cloak a bit of a shake; it's raining very hard.'

Sir Oliver was surprised when the *molto reverendo parocco* came out into the passage to meet him; he had never seen such a small priest before; when he bowed he had to bend so low that the blood flowed into his head.

'That will do,' said the priest. 'I am only a Franciscan, *cavaliere*. They call me Padre Ippolito. *Hé*, Marietta, bring sausage and wine. This way, sir, it's terribly dark just here. You are *Inglese*, is it not so? There, you see, since you English broke away from the holy church of Rome there are swarms of you in Italy. I understand, *signore*. You must be homesick for it. Poor boy, so young and an Englishman already! Cut yourself some of this sausage, *cavaliere*, it is genuine Veronese. I always say there is nothing like Veronese sausage for bringing out the flavour of wine, let the Bolognese stuff themselves with their mortadello if they like. You stick to Veronese sausage and salted almonds, my dear son. Have you been in Verona? No? A pity. It was the birthplace of the divine Paolo Veronese, *signore*. I am a native of Verona myself. A famous city, sir. They call it the city of the Scaligeri. Is this wine to your taste?'

'*Grazie*, Padre,' stammered Sir Oliver. 'In England we call Verona the city of Juliet.'

'Fancy that,' said Padre Ippolito surprised, 'and why? I didn't even know that a Princess Juliet lived there. But of course I haven't been there for over forty years. Which Juliet would that be?'

'Juliet Capulet,' Sir Oliver explained. 'You see we have a play about her – by a man called Shakespeare. A beautiful play. Do you know it, Padre?'

'No. But wait a minute, Juliet Capulet, Juliet Capulet,'

murmured Padre Ippolito, 'I ought to know her. I used to be at the Capulets' place with Father Laurence.'

'You knew Friar Laurence?' exclaimed Sir Oliver.

'Of course I knew him! Why, I was his server. Listen, would it be the Juliet who married Count Paris? I knew her. A most pious and excellent lady, the Countess Juliet. She was a Capulet by birth, one of the Capulets who had the velvet business.'

'That can't be the one,' declared Sir Oliver. 'The real Juliet died while still a girl in the most touching manner that you can imagine.'

'Aha,' said the *molto reverendo*, 'then it wasn't the same one. The Juliet I knew married the Count Paris and had eight children by him. A model and virtuous wife, young sir, may God give you one like her. It's true there was a rumour that before that she had lost her head about some young scapegrace – Eh, *signore*, isn't there something of the sort to be said about all of us? Youth, we know, is hot-headed and heedless. Be glad that you are young, *cavaliere*. Are the English all young?'

'Yes,' declared Sir Oliver. 'Ah, Father, we too are consumed with the same fire as young Romeo.'

'Romeo?' asked Padre Ippolito, and took a pull at his wine. 'I seem to know that name. Why, wasn't he that young *sciocco*, that scamp, that scoundrel of the house of Montague who stabbed Count Paris? People said it was about Juliet. Yes, that was it. Juliet was going to marry Count Paris – it was a good match, *signore*, Paris was very rich and a nice young man – but Romeo made out that Juliet was to have married him. Such nonsense, sir,' snorted the priest. 'As though the rich Capulets could give their daughter to one of the Montagues, who had come down in the world. And besides, the Montagues took the side of Mantua while the Capulets were on the side of the

Duke of Milan. No, no. I think the *assalto assassinatico* against Paris was just an ordinary political crime. There's politics in everything in these days, my dear son. Of course, after an outrage like that Romeo had to flee to Mantua and he never came back again.'

'Oh, but that isn't true!' burst out Sir Oliver. 'Forgive me, Padre, but it wasn't like that at all. Juliet loved Romeo but her parents forced her to marry Count Paris –'

'They had good reasons,' agreed the old priest. 'Romeo was a *ribaldo* and hand in glove with the Mantuan party.'

'But before her marriage with Paris Father Laurence gave her a potion to send her into a death-like sleep,' went on Sir Oliver.

'That's a lie,' said Padre Ippolito sharply. 'Father Laurence would never have done such a thing. But it is true that Romeo attacked Paris in the street and wounded him. Perhaps he was drunk.'

'Forgive me, Father, but it was quite different,' protested Sir Oliver. 'What really happened was that they buried Juliet. Romeo ran Paris through with his sword and killed him on her grave –'

'Stop a minute,' said the priest. 'In the first place it wasn't on her grave but in the street near the monument of the Scaligeri. And, secondly, Romeo didn't pierce him to the heart but only ran him through the shoulder. It isn't as easy as all that to kill a man with your sword. Just you try it, young man.'

'*Scusi*,' objected Sir Oliver, 'but I saw it on the stage at the very first performance. Count Paris was really run through in the duel and died on the spot. Romeo, in the belief that Juliet was really dead, poisoned himself in her tomb. That's how it was, Padre.'

'Not a bit of it,' growled Father Ippolito. 'He didn't poison himself. He ran away to Mantua, my friend.'

'Forgive me, Padre,' persisted Oliver, 'I saw it with my own eyes – why, I was sitting in the front row! At that moment Juliet waked up and when she saw that her beloved Romeo was dead, she took poison as well and died.'

'You've got it quite wrong,' said Padre Ippolito indignantly. 'I cannot think who invented these rumours. The truth is that Romeo ran away to Mantua and poor little Juliet was heartbroken about it and did try to poison herself. But it was nothing, *cavaliere*, just a piece of childishness; why, she was hardly fifteen years old. I know about it from Friar Laurence, young man; of course I was only a *ragazzo* about so high at the time,' the good father held out his hand about eighteen inches from the ground. 'Then they took Juliet to her aunt at Bezenzano to get well again. Count Paris went there to see her; he still had his arm in a sling and you know what happens in such cases: she fell head over heels in love with him. They were married three months later. *Ecco, signore,* that's the way things are in life. I was server at her wedding in a white *cotta*,'

Sir Oliver sat as though overwhelmed. 'Forgive me, Father,' he said at last, 'but it's a thousand times more beautiful in the English play.'

Padre Ippolito snorted. 'Beautiful! I don't know what you find beautiful about two young people taking their own lives. It would have been a sad business, young man. I tell you, it is more beautiful that Juliet married and had eight children – and what children! As pretty as pictures!'

Oliver shook his head. 'It's not that, dear Father; you don't know what a great love is like.'

The little priest blinked thoughtfully. 'A great love? I think that is when two people manage to live together in unity all through their lives ... devotedly and faithfully ... Juliet was a rare and noble lady, my dear sir. She brought up eight children and loved her husband devotedly to the end of her days.

'So you call Verona the city of Juliet? That is extraordinarily nice of you English, *cavaliere*. Lady Juliet was truly an excellent woman, may God grant her eternal glory.'

Young Oliver pulled himself out of a fit of abstraction. 'And what happened to Romeo?'

'Him? I really don't know. I did hear some rumour about him. – Ah, now I remember. He fell in love in Mantua with the daughter of some marquis or other – what was he called? Monfalcone. Montefalco, or something like that. Ah, *cavaliere*, that was what you call a great love! In the end he ran away with her or something – it was a highly romantic story but I have forgotten the details; you see, it happened in Mantua. But it was supposed to be a *passione senza esempio*, an overwhelming passion, sir. At least that's what they said. *Ecco, signore,* the rain has stopped.'

Sir Oliver rose to his full and embarrassing height. 'You've been awfully kind, Padre. Thank you so much. Perhaps I may leave something here ... for your poor parishioners,' he stammered, reddening and stuffing a handful of *zecchini* under the edge of his plate.

'No, no,' protested Padre Ippolito flapping his hands, 'you mustn't really – all that money just for a little bit of Verona sausage!'

'Some of it is for your story,' said Oliver quickly. 'It was – er, it was very – I really don't know what to call it. Simply amazing.'

The sun streamed in at the windows of the priest's house.

(1932)

Master Hynek Rab of Kufstejn

MASTER Janek Chval of Jankov had not yet recovered from his surprise. His son-in-law had suddenly burst in on him out of the blue for a visit, and what a son-in-law, just look at him! He wore German breeches and Hungarian moustaches; quite a fine gentleman and that's the truth; and there was old Master Janek with his sleeves rolled up helping to deliver a cow that was calving. This is a nice business, thought the old man irritably, what the devil has he come for?

'Have a drink, Master Hynek,' he urged him warmly. 'It's only a local wine, a Jew from Litomerice brought it five years ago. You drink Cyprian wine in Prague, don't you?'

'One kind and another,' answered Hynek. 'But I tell you this, father-in-law, there's nothing to beat an honest Czech wine. And good Czech beer, sir. The folk where I come from don't know how good our own things are and they buy all sorts of foreign trash. As if anyone brought us anything really good from abroad.'

The old man nodded his head. 'And the unchristian price they ask for it.'

'Of course,' said Rab, piling it on. 'Just take the duties, for instance. His Gracious Majesty lines his pockets and we have to pay out.' Master Rab spat angrily. 'Just for *him* to have coffers full of money!'

'George of Podiebrady?'

'That little tich,' agreed Rab. 'He looks like a grocer. A

pretty sort of king we've got, what? But things are chang-
ing, father-in-law. For economic reasons and such-like. Are
things as bad with you here in Jankov?'

Master Janek looked gloomy. 'Bad, my boy. Things are
bad here. A murrain has struck the cattle, smoking out the
cow-houses is no use. The corn is hit with the blight, the
devil knows why. Last year we had hail. – It's bad for the
peasants. Just think, Master Hynek, they hadn't even
grain for sowing. I had to give them seed corn from my
own barn –'

'You gave it them?' asked Master Rab surprised. 'I
wouldn't have done that, father-in-law. Why pamper the
lazy churls? If they can't manage to make a living, let
them die. Let them die,' he repeated energetically. 'What
we need today is the iron hand. No charity and no dole. It
only makes them soft! Worse times are coming. These
beggars had better get used to a little poverty. Let them eat
bark and things like that. I wouldn't have given them anything; I'd just have said to them straight out: You
beggarly ruffians, you impudent clodhoppers and so on.
Do you think we've nothing more serious to worry about
than what you're going to eat? Today, I'd have said to
them, we must all be prepared to make great sacrifices. We
must think of defending our kingdom and nothing less
than that. That's what I'd have said to them. The times
are serious and anyone who isn't prepared to give his life
for his country must die of hunger. And that's that.'
Master Hynek took a long pull at his wine. 'Drill them as
long as they can stand on their feet, and no words wasted.'

Old Master Janek stared blankly at his son-in-law with
his pale eyes. 'What's that? what's that?' he stammered
in perplexity. 'Do you mean – God forbid! – that there's
going to be war?'

Master Hynek broke into a long peal of laughter. 'Of

course! There must be. Do we have peace for nothing? Ah, Master, when there's peace it's only reasonable that something's brewing. Now I ask you,' he went on scornfully, 'why, the fellow knows it himself – what do they call him? eh? the peaceful prince! The peaceful prince,' Master Rab burst out. 'It's obvious he's afraid for his throne. No one would even see him if he didn't sit on a throne with three cushions under his behind.'

'D'you mean Podiebrady?' asked Janek doubtfully.

'Who else? Eh, Master, a nice ruler we've got! Nothing but peace, father-in-law. Nothing but embassies and things like that. That's what the money's for, you know. Look here – he went trapesing right over to Hlohovec after the Polish king about a pact against the Turks, or so they say. He went a whole mile to meet the Poles! Think of it! What do you say to that?'

'Well,' said Master Janek cautiously. 'They had to talk about the Turks, didn't they?'

'That's all nonsense,' said Hynek Rab firmly. 'Is it fitting that a Czech king should do honour to a Pole? It's disgraceful!' he shouted. 'He ought to have waited till the Pole came to him! To think it's come to that, Master Janek! What would the late Emperor Charles say to it, or Sigismund? In those days, my dear sir, we still had a certain international prestige –' Master Rab spat. 'Faugh! I'm surprised we Czechs put up with such dishonour.'

It's all very tiresome, thought Master Janek Chval fretfully. And why does he want to tell it to me? As if I hadn't enough worries of my own?

'Or this,' continued Rab pontifically, '– he sends an embassy to Rome for the Pope to recognize him or something like that. Asks him nice and politely, you know. So that there may be peace in Christendom, he says, and all

the rest of it. It really beats everything!' Master Rab
banged his fist on the table, nearly knocking over his
tankard. 'It's enough to make old Žižka turn in his grave!
Negotiations with the Pope! Did you ever hear the like?
Is this what we of the Protestant faith have bled for? For
him to sell us to Rome for one of the Pope's slippers?'

Why are you carrying on about it so, wondered the old
man, blinking absent-mindedly. When have you bled for
anything? Your late father only came over with Sigismund. Yes, then he married into a Prague family. He wrote
his name Joachim Hanes Raab. He was an excellent fellow,
that he was, I knew him; a very sensible German.

'And he thinks,' went on Hynek Rab, working himself
up, 'that he's engaging in some sort of high politics. He's
sent one of his mountebanks right over to France, to see
the French king. Says he wants to found a league of
Christian princes who are to meet in a sort of pan-
European conference, or something like that. To settle
disputes and so on. And against the Turk and for ever-
lasting peace and I don't know what. Now I ask you, did
you ever in your life hear such nonsense? A pretty way
of carrying on politics, isn't it? Who's going to settle disputes by peaceful means when they can be settled by
war? As if any state would let herself be talked round
when it wants to have a war with another? Just nonsense;
the whole world is simply laughing about it. But what
about us, father-in-law? Doesn't this weak step com-
promise us before the whole world? Why, great heavens,
it makes us look as if we were afraid of war breaking out
against us –'

'And will it?' asked Master Janek anxiously.

Master Hynek Rab of Kufstejn nodded his head. 'You
can take your Bible oath on it. Look here, father-in-law,

we've got Hungary, the Germans, the Pope and Austria all against us. Very well, we must attack them before they have time to unite. War at once and have done with it. That's the thing to do,' declared Rab, stroking his hair in a resolute manner.

'I'd better see about laying in stores in time,' muttered Master Janek Chval thoughtfully. 'It's a good thing to have provisions laid by.'

Master Hynek Rab leaned across the table confidentially. 'I've got a better plan. Unite with the Turks and the Tartars. That would be policy, what? Leave Poland and Germany to the Tartars. Let them destroy and burn everything there. All the better for us, d'you see? And leave Hungary, Austria and the Pope to the Turks.'

'They say the Turk is a monster,' grunted the old man.

'Exactly,' admitted Master Hynek. 'He'd settle their hash ! But let's stop beating about the bush and all this business of Christian feelings ! It's simply a question of power. And our country, sir – I always say that no sacrifice is too great to make for our country; but the others must make it, you see. No slackers, as our Žižka used to say. Let them all come ! If only there were more genuine and true-hearted patriots ! Just let's lay about us again with our time-honoured Czech clubs –'

Master Janek Chval of Jankov nodded his head. I must remember to lay in stores, he thought. One never knows what may happen. Old Master Raab was a wise man, though he was as German as they're made. A Tyrolese. Hynek may have inherited a bit of his sense, thought the old man, and in Prague folk know all sorts of things – I must dry a lot of hay. They need hay in war time.

Master Hynek Rab of Kufstejn banged the table cheerfully with his fist. 'Master father-in-law, we shall see what we shall see ! Your health ! Hey, boy, here with that jug !

Pour me out some wine! Don't you see there's an empty flagon in front of me? Here's to our cause!'

'*Wohl bekomm's*,' responded old Master Janek courteously.

(1933)

Napoleon

MADEMOISELLE Claire of the Comédie Française sat
without stirring a finger; she knew that the emperor sometimes had fits of abstraction like this and did not care to
be disturbed. Besides, *entre nous*, what could one talk to
him about? *Que voulez-vous?* He was just the emperor; one
did not feel really at home with him, *pas vrai?* (After all,
he's a foreigner, thought Mademoiselle Claire, *pas très
parisien*.) All the same, his face was handsome enough in
the firelight. (If only he weren't so fat.) (*La la*, he's got no
neck, *c'est drôle*.) (But you know, he might be a little
more polite!)

The heavy marble clock ticked on the mantelpiece. Tomorrow, thought the emperor, I must receive the repre-
sentatives of the towns – it's stupid, but *que faire?* They'll
certainly complain about the taxes. Then the Austrian
Ambassador – it's always the same story. After that the
new presidents of the courts are coming to be presented –
I must read up before then where each of them has been
working; it pleases them when I know something about
them. He counted on his fingers. Something else? Yes,
Conte Ventura, he'll talk about the Pope again – Napoleon
suppressed a yawn. *Dieu*, what a bore! I ought to send
for that – what's his name? – that clever fellow who's
just come back from England. Whatever is the man's
name? – *porco*, and he's my best spy!

'Sacrebleu,' grumbled the emperor, 'what is the fellow's
name?'

Mademoiselle Claire moved a little further away and remained sympathetically silent.

It doesn't matter, thought the emperor; I don't care what his name is, but his information is first rate. An indispensable fellow, that – that – *maledetto*! Stupid the way one couldn't think of names sometimes! And yet I've a good memory for names, he thought. How many thousands of them do I carry in my head? – only think of the soldiers whom I know by name! I'll wager that I can still remember the names of all my fellow cadets at the military academy – and my playfellows when I was a child. Let's see, there was Tonio, called Biglia, Francio alias Riccintello, Tonio Zufolo, Mario Barbabietola, Luca, called Peto (the emperor smiled), Andrea who was called Puzzo or Tirone ... I can remember all their names and now I can't remember the name of that fellow – *tonnerre*!

'Madame,' he said, absorbed in his subject, 'have you got a queer sort of memory too? One can remember the names of all one's playmates as a child but not of a fellow one spoke to only a month ago.'

'Exactly, Sire,' said Mademoiselle Claire. 'It's strange, isn't it?' She tried to remember the names of some of her playmates but none occurred to her; she only remembered her first lover. He was someone called Henri. Yes, Henri, that was it.

'Queer,' muttered the emperor, staring into the flaming hearth. 'I can call them all up before me. Gamba, Zufolo, Briccone, Barbabietola, little Puzzo, Biglia, Mattaccio, Mazzasette, Beccajo, Ciondolone, Panciuto – There were about twenty of us young scamps, Madame. They called me Polio, *il capitano*.'

'Charming,' exclaimed Mademoiselle Claire. 'And you, Sire, were their captain?'

'Of course,' said the emperor thoughtfully. 'I was

captain of the robber band or of the soldiers, according to circumstances. I led them, you see. Once I even gave orders to hang Mattaccio for disobedience. Yes, yes; but the old watchman, Zoppo, cut him down in time. We ruled differently in those days, Madame. A *capitano* was absolute master of his people. There was a gang of boys who were our enemies, it was led by a boy called Zani. Later he actually became a brigand chief in Corsica. Three years ago I had him shot.'

'It is obvious that Your Majesty was a born leader,' breathed Mademoiselle Claire.

The emperor shook his head. 'You think so? In those days as *capitano* I felt my own power far more strongly. Governing, Madame, is not like commanding. To command without doubts or questionings – heedless of possible consequences – Madame, the sovereign part of the whole thing was that it was only a game, that I knew it was only a game –'

Mademoiselle Claire divined that there was nothing to say to this; she hoped it would be set down to her credit.

'And it's the same even now,' he went on more or less to himself. 'I often get the sudden thought; Polio, of course it's only a game! They call you Sire, they call you Your Majesty because we're playing at it, all of us. The soldiers at attention – the ministers and ambassadors bowing to the ground – it's all a game. And no one nudges his neighbour, no one begins to laugh. As children we played seriously like that. It's part of the game, Madame: to pretend that it's all real –'

The heavy marble clock ticked away on the mantelpiece. The emperor is queer, thought Mademoiselle Claire uncomfortably.

'Perhaps they wink at each other behind closed doors,'

he went on, absorbed. 'Perhaps they whisper to each other: "He's a wag, that Polio, the way he plays at being emperor and never bats an eyelid – if it weren't a game you'd think he took it seriously!"' He gave a snort as if he were laughing inside. 'Comic, isn't it, Madame? And I have my eye on them too – so as to be the *first* to burst out laughing when they begin nudging each other. But they never do. Sometimes I have the feeling that they are conspiring to make a fool of me. You understand? to make me believe it *isn't* a game – and then they'd laugh at me: Polio, Polio, now we've caught you!' He laughed softly to himself. 'No, no! They won't catch me! I know what I know –'

Polio, thought Mademoiselle Claire to herself. When he is tender I'll call him that. Polio. *Mon petit* Polio.

'I beg your pardon?' said the emperor sharply.

'Nothing, Sire,' answered Mademoiselle Claire on her guard.

'Indeed? I thought you said something.' He leaned towards the fire. 'It's odd, I haven't noticed it with women; but with men it happens fairly often. Deep down inside they never stop being little boys. That's why they do so much harm in life, they're really only playing. That's why they do things with such passionate concentration, because it's really a game. Don't you think so? As if one could seriously be an emperor! I know it's all a hoax.'

There was silence. 'No, no, no,' he murmured. 'Don't believe it. But sometimes one isn't sure, you know. One gets a sudden scare – why, I'm still only little Polio and all this is just pretending, isn't it? But *mon Dieu*, when it explodes! *That's* really the thing, one can't be certain –' He raised his eyes and stared at Mademoiselle Claire. 'It is only with women, Madame, only in love that one's sure that – that – that one's no longer a child; then at least one knows one's a man, *que diable*!' He sprang to his feet. '*Allons*, Madame!'

He was suddenly very passionate and ruthless.

'Ah, Sire,' breathed Mademoiselle Claire, '*comme vous êtes grand*!'

(1933)